COPY 1   1895

VOICES

AFTER

MIDNIGHT

Also by Richard Peck

NOVELS FOR YOUNG PEOPLE

DON'T LOOK AND IT WON'T
  HURT
DREAMLAND LAKE
THROUGH A BRIEF DARKNESS
REPRESENTING SUPER DOLL
THE GHOST BELONGED TO ME
GHOSTS I HAVE BEEN
ARE YOU IN THE HOUSE
  ALONE?
FATHER FIGURE
SECRETS OF THE SHOPPING
  MALL

CLOSE ENOUGH TO TOUCH
THE DREADFUL FUTURE OF
  BLOSSOM CULP
REMEMBERING THE GOOD
  TIMES
BLOSSOM CULP AND THE
  SLEEP OF DEATH
PRINCESS ASHLEY
THOSE SUMMER GIRLS I
  NEVER MET

NOVELS FOR ADULTS

AMANDA/MIRANDA
NEW YORK TIME
THIS FAMILY OF WOMEN

PICTURE BOOKS

MONSTER NIGHT AT GRANDMA'S HOUSE
(ILLUSTRATED BY DON FREEMAN)

NONFICTION ANTHOLOGIES

EDGE OF AWARENESS (COEDITED WITH NED E. HOOPES)
LEAP INTO REALITY

VERSE ANTHOLOGIES

SOUNDS AND SILENCES
MINDSCAPES
PICTURES THAT STORM INSIDE MY HEAD

Richard Peck

VOICES
AFTER
MIDNIGHT

A Novel

Delacorte Press

Published by
Delacorte Press
Bantam Doubleday Dell Publishing Group, Inc.
666 Fifth Avenue
New York, New York 10103

Library of Congress Cataloging in Publication Data
Peck, Richard [date of birth]
    Voices after midnight / by Richard Peck.
        p.   cm.
    Summary: Living with their sister and parents in a rented house in New York City during the summer, Chad and Luke uncover a mystery involving the former tenants of the house when the two brothers slip back in time to 1888.
    ISBN 0-385-29779-3
    [1. Time travel—Fiction.   2. Brothers and sisters—Fiction. 3. New York (N.Y.)—Fiction.]   I. Title.
    PZ.P338Vo   1989
    [Fic]—dc19   89-1099
                                                                      CIP
                                                                       AC

Manufactured in the United States of America

September 1989

10   9   8   7   6   5   4   3   2   1

BG

For Phyllis Whitney

VOICES

AFTER

MIDNIGHT

One

In my usual dream I'm riding a Honda Gyro. I've got on big boots, and I'm thundering through the nights down interstate highways with the wind whistling in my crash helmet. My shirttail's flapping under my flight jacket, and I'm sitting on a lot of horsepower. And that Gyro is mine. Look, I'm fourteen. I can dream, can't I?

But for many nights before we went to New York, my dream-machine moped was nowhere in sight. Instead, I dreamed about snow. The minute my head hit the pillow, I was up to here in white drifts. It was like drowning in frozen yogurt, cool and smooth and standing up in peaks. And here in California, we don't see much snow except on the slopes.

One morning when I woke up from a blizzard dream, my sister Heidi was standing down at the foot of my bed. She'd reached in under the sheet and had one of my big toes in a death grip.

"Chad, get up. Like now. It's after ten."

My toe was coming out of its socket, and it really shook the snowflakes out of my head. I could either hop out of bed on the other foot, or I could be in a corrective shoe for the rest of my life.

Heidi had been in a bad mood for weeks because she really didn't want to go to New York with the rest of us.

But I thought she and I had a deal. We never go into each other's room unless the house is on fire. I played for time. After all, summer vacation had already started.

"I'm only wearing underpants," I said.

"Do I care?" Heidi was jingling something in her other hand. Mom's car keys.

"Where's Mom?" I said.

"Out." Heidi smiled. "She's doing some last-minute shopping with Mrs. Ackerman. In Mrs. Ackerman's car."

I began to see. "Where's Luke?"

Heidi freed my toe. "He's been up for hours. Now he's just waiting around for something to do."

I doubted that. My little brother Luke keeps busy. He may have more inner resources than any eight-year-old needs.

We used to be this family with a mom and a dad, two brothers, and a sister. Then Heidi hit high school, and we became a mom, a dad, two brothers, and an alien. Ever since ninth grade Heidi's wanted to be either on the phone or on the road. But she only has a learner's permit. She can't get a real driver's license till her birthday in the fall. That meant she couldn't drive a car without a responsible adult in the seat next to her. A brave responsible adult.

"We're going for a drive." She tucked a few strands of her long hair behind an ear. She's blond like Mom.

It's been a couple of semesters since Heidi's even

wanted to be seen in public with Luke and me. I wondered where we were going. Not to the mall where we might run into Mom—literally. And that only left—

"Melissa's house," Heidi said. "I've got to go over and see her on a life-or-death matter." Heidi's eyes got big and blue like Mom's. Melissa Schultz is her best friend forever. They'd probably been on the phone a couple of times this morning already.

"You and Luke and I . . . ought to do more stuff together."

Also, though I'm not a responsible adult, she could use all the help she could get driving Mom's car. "I hate to say it, Heidi, but being in a car with you at the wheel could be hazardous to my health."

Heidi sighed. "We'll take side streets. It's ten minutes there, ten minutes back. Piece of cake."

Anyway, she'd already talked me into it. Would I miss a ride with Heidi as pilot? It could be more exciting than Magic Mountain. Then we couldn't find Luke. He doesn't come when you call him because his mind's on other things. We looked all over, even in the living room, where nobody goes except on national holidays.

There's a picture of Mom in the living room, a big one Dad put up over the fireplace. It's the year she was Rose Queen down in Pasadena at the Rose Bowl game. She doesn't say what year. In the picture Mom's in a white Chrysler Imperial convertible, carrying a big bouquet of red roses. She's wearing a crown, and her smile's sensational. Heidi tries to avoid looking at this picture. Anyway, Luke was nowhere to be seen.

We finally found him in his own walk-in closet, down on the floor talking to Al. I don't know about talking, but they seemed to communicate. Al's a dog—Victoria Alexandrina, but we call her Al. She's mainly Luke's dog, a pug with a typical pushed-in pug face. But she has a good champagne coat, and her tail wraps in a tight curl because she has a really good pedigree.

"Better than ours," Dad always says.

Luke and Al were down on the closet floor, communicating. Luke was wearing his Freddy Krueger mask just for kicks, and Al was staring around with her big bulgy glass eyes. A fairly weird scene, but typical.

"I'm never having any kids," Heidi said.

I lifted off the Freddy mask, and there was Luke, blond like the rest of us with a pointy chin and prominent ears. He was just sitting there, cross-legged with his small hands on his bare knees.

"Hey, Luke, want to go for a ride?"

He blinked. "Who's driving?"

But he wouldn't have missed it either. The only one who didn't get to go was Al.

Mom's dream machine, the Taurus, was already out there on the drive. It's the four-cam, twenty-four-valve version of Ford's V-6 with 220 horses under the hood. The thought of all that power in Heidi's hands slowed me down, but we all piled in. Luke went in the back, and I buckled up.

It was a hundred and ten degrees in the car, but Heidi's cool. She tucked her hair behind both ears, flipped the ignition, and the Taurus gunned in neutral. I could feel Luke's breath on the back of my neck.

"Just show me reverse," Heidi said, "and I'll be fine."

Out in the street I had to show her drive. Then we jerked away over the curving streets of the El Rancho Bravo subdivision. Our house is one of the Estrellita models, your basic trilevel. Six hundred Estrellitas were built in Phase One of El Rancho Bravo, so when you visit the neighbors, you feel right at home.

But the Schultzes lived across the route in Fremont Acres. At the big intersection I pointed Heidi into the lane heading for Melissa's house. Otherwise we'd have peeled off in the wrong direction and could have ended up in Fresno, even Mexico. Somehow she bumped the turn signal with her elbow, so we seemed to be making a permanent right-hand turn for the rest of the trip. But I let that go.

As we rolled through the gates of Fremont Acres, Heidi settled back. She was picturing herself as seventeen at least. She even looked over and gave me a small smile.

The Schultzes' house is at the top of a rise, instant Spanish with several wings. They have a curving drive two lanes wide, which was lucky for Heidi. Up under the arcade at the front of the house was Mrs. Schultz's new Cadillac Allante.

But Luke wasn't interested. He pointed a finger past

my ear. "What's that?" He meant an old house next door to the Schultzes'. It would have been there before the subdivision, a farmhouse. Though it was run-down, the lawn was neat and full of flower beds.

Heidi shuddered. She'd slowed to a creep, getting ready to make a right-hand turn at last.

"That's the witchwoman's house," she said. "We've never seen her, but she is *so mean*. The Schultzes can't pipe any music outdoors or have a pool party after midnight. If they do, the witchwoman calls the police. Can you believe it?"

I could, but Luke was hanging over the seat, staring at the farmhouse like it was the only good thing in the area. He likes anything old.

Heidi wheeled into the Schultzes' drive, and we lurched to a halt. I pointed to park, and she shifted into it. I pointed to the keys, and she pulled them out of the ignition.

Melissa met us at the front door. She and Heidi were wearing matching jumpsuits in camouflage colors, so, yes, they'd been on the phone this morning. "Guess what?" Melissa said to her. "Mom's gone *shopping*, and we're *alone*."

So they did a little dance then, a cross between cheer-leading and something Native American.

"Hi, Chad," Melissa said, looking just over my head. "Hi, Tim," she said to Luke.

"Luke," I said.

"Whatever," Melissa said.

We all trooped out to the Schultzes' kitchen, which was quite a trip. Melissa brought out four frosty cans of Slice and a box of doughnuts. She and Heidi climbed on a couple of stools and got down to serious planning. A lot of it was in their own kind of shorthand talk, but I already knew what it was about.

We were going to spend two weeks in New York because Dad's firm was calling him back to reorganize their Manhattan office. He's with Esterhazy, Cranshaw, & Phipps Advertising, on the noncreative side. When Heidi heard she'd have to be away from Melissa and California for two weeks of summer vacation, she started campaigning to stay behind with the Schultzes.

". . . and better yet," Melissa was saying, "my mother will be away for practically the *whole two weeks*. She's going to that ashram-type spa down at Calabasas."

She and Heidi both screamed then and did a sitting-down cheer routine.

I wondered if Mom and Dad would let Heidi stay behind with the Schultzes. She had an excellent record for getting her way.

"But the best thing is Something Else!" Melissa said. Their heads got closer, so it had to be about guys. Melissa seemed to know a guy who might take Heidi to the mall if she was going to be around.

He was a River Phoenix look-alike, old enough for a real driver's license, had his own Acura Integra, and partied in Palm Springs. A hunk. The more I eavesdropped, the more I thought Melissa had lifted him out of a Harlequin Romance. For one thing, his name was Thor Desmond.

By now Heidi was spinning around on the stool, and her hair was standing straight out. But Luke was getting bored. He was over by the French windows that looked out on the Schultzes' pool. I strolled over. He was looking wise as always, and there was doughnut glaze all over his mouth. When he slipped his hand into mine, it was still cold from the Slice can.

"Too much girl-talk," he said. "Let's get some fresh air."

We went out the back way, and we weren't missed. The day was heating up, and I thought he might want to go down and check out the pool. They had one of those robots that clean the pool by themselves, which I thought he might like.

But he didn't. We strolled around the Schultzes' garden, which was pretty nice. When he saw a gap in the hedge, we both slipped through. It was cooler on the other side. We were behind the witchwoman's house, which didn't worry Luke. He stood there, getting his bearings.

The witchwoman had a good piece of property. The backyard was more natural than the front, with a lot of native California plants. She'd let some bright bottlebrush bushes grow wild. The big shade trees made shadowy patterns. The farther back we went, the wilder it was, not even mowed. I noticed something.

There was an old shanty or something back there. I'd almost missed seeing it. It wasn't there, and then it was. Luke was looking up at me, watching me.

He gave me a tug, and we walked back to the little house behind the bottle-brush bushes. A cabin, definitely a lot older than the big house, stood back there. It was made out of logs and loose stones. The roof was hand-split cedar shingles. It was really old-fashioned, with firewood on the porch. An old-time pan hung on a nail by the door.

We were way back from the street here, so maybe that's why it was so quiet. You couldn't hear anything—traffic or people splashing in their pools. It was completely silent, except for birds, and I didn't see any.

"Maybe we better not—"

"It's okay," Luke said.

We went up on the porch. You could smell fresh sawdust like this place wasn't as old as it looked. There was no knob on the door, just a leather thong arrangement. Luke eased up the latch, and the door swung open. There was a potbellied stove in one corner. Otherwise, not a lot of furniture: a bed with rope springs and the bedroll rolled up, a shelf with some antique baking-powder cans. Clothes hung on pegs, and a blue coffee-pot stood on the stove.

"This is great," I said. "You know what this is supposed to be?"

Luke nodded. "It's a prospector's cabin from back in

the Gold Rush days. Around 1849 or 1850. This was gold country, you know."

"And look at the condition," I said. "It's mint. This ought to be in Knott's Berry Farm or somewhere."

Luke rubbed his chin. "We probably ought to be getting back," he said, which isn't the kind of thing you expect to hear from an eight-year-old.

"What's the hurry?"

"The prospector could come back," he said.

So we had a laugh about that. At least I did.

"In a way it was kind of spooky," I said when we were back on the Schultzes' side of the hedge. We'd returned to a world of birdbaths and high-grade plastic lawn furniture. "You think the witchwoman next door really is a witch?"

"Naw," Luke said. "There aren't any. Girls Heidi's age think all grown-up ladies are witches. It's a stage girls go through."

And of course he had a point. It was definitely time to get going. Heidi was out on the Schultzes' back patio having a fit.

"Where have you two dweebs been?" She came running up to us. She'd have knocked our heads together if we'd been the same height. "We've got to get out of here. Do you know what Melissa just told me? Her mom's at the mall, and she's with Mrs. Ackerman *too*. Our mom, her mom—all of them."

"So?"

"They're all three in Mrs. Ackerman's car, and she's

going to drop them off, and they're due back like *now.* They could pull up in Melissa's drive any *second.* Mom could be home *already."*

If so, she'd be wondering where her Taurus went. And when she found out, Heidi wouldn't have a hope of staying with the Schultzes while the rest of us went to New York. We sprinted through the Schultzes' house. Melissa skipped on ahead, opened the front door, and we all shot through.

Fortunately, Mrs. Ackerman's BMW with three heads in it wasn't coming up the drive behind the Taurus. Heidi was moving faster than I'd ever seen her move. But while Luke and I scrambled into the car, she hung back for one last word with Melissa.

"Okay, Melissa, this is the bottom line," Heidi was saying. "If I can't stay with you, *and* meet Thor Desmond, then the rest of my life is a total wipeout, right?"

"Right," Melissa said.

Heidi was in the car now, digging around for the keys. "I've lost them," she said. "No, here they are."

I pointed to the ignition, and she tried to start it with the trunk key. Then she got the right one. "Listen, Melissa, this is crucial. We can't let *anything* spoil our plans, okay?"

"Okay," Melissa said.

Then something bad happened. Heidi banged her door shut, and the car roared in park. I showed her drive, and, boy, did she. She was nervous, and she really needed to get home. So she jammed her Reebok down

on the accelerator, really floorboarded it. It was like
rocket science. I was pinned against my headrest, and
Luke seemed to do a somersault on the backseat. A pair
of Mom's big sunglasses and the visor she wears on the
tennis court jumped off the top of the dash and landed
in my lap. We shot forward on the Schultzes' curving
drive. But we went straight.

Straight off the drive and across the lawn. A Taurus
can get up to forty miles an hour before you have time
to hide your eyes. We were gunning over the Schultzes'
golf-green grass. The witchwoman's shade trees were
looming up. The entire world was a blur.

"Where's . . ."

Where's the brake is what Heidi wondered, but it was
hard to think. I'd buckled up, but now I wanted out,
and Luke too. We blasted between two trees, and the
witchwoman's best flower bed was right there at the
end of our hood. I had my door unlatched but couldn't
get it open. Luke was halfway over my headrest and
scrambling. Then Heidi remembered the handbrake.
She yanked it so hard, it nearly came off in her hand. I
bumped the gearshift into park and peeled out the
door. Luke and I ended up in a pile on the lawn. The
Taurus was halfway into the flower bed. There were
these neat rows of waxy begonias: red then white then
the front wheels of the Taurus, dug in. For part of a
second Heidi rested her head on the steering wheel.

I was up, brushing off Luke and checking him for
damage. Then Heidi was out of the door on her side.

"Now you boys really must get back into the car at once," she said, loud and in a real strange voice. "Do as Mother says."

I looked across the hood, and she was standing there with her hair scooped suddenly up in Mom's sun visor. She'd put on Mom's big sunglasses, which really disguised her. As Mom.

"What next?" Luke said in a small voice.

I looked up at the witchwoman's house, and her front door was opening. Heidi disguising herself as Mom was quicker reasoning than I'd have given her credit for. But it was definitely time to be running along.

"It was all I could think of," she said, panting as we all piled back in the car. I showed her reverse, and we shot backward, out of the begonias and by a miracle between the trees.

"Take it easy, Heidi," I said, because I didn't know you could reverse this fast. We bumped back onto the Schultzes' drive, and we could have terminated Melissa except she seemed to be back in her house behind a locked door.

Heidi found the brake on the floor and hit it. I caught a glimpse of our tire tracks across two lawns and into the flower bed. There seemed to be somebody coming down off the witchwoman's front porch, heading our way. Heidi found drive all by herself, and we laid rubber all the way down the Schultzes' drive. She signaled right and made a sharp left into the street. And we were out of there.

Nobody spoke all the way through Fremont Acres. We stopped at a light at the big intersection. Heidi flipped off Mom's tennis visor. I looked around to check on Luke. He had both feet braced against the backs of our seats, and his eyes were really big.

"Well, so much for my summer," Heidi said, whipping off the big glasses. "I've blown it. I'll be lucky if Mom doesn't find out about this."

You've got that right, I thought, but didn't say so.

"Of course, Melissa would never tell on me."

Don't count on it, I thought silently.

"And how can I stay with the Schultzes now? The witchwoman could track me down and have the law on me."

She might even have a make on our plates. But I didn't say so because it sounded too much like TV.

"I may have to go away somewhere and start a whole new life. I could end up with my picture in post offices around here." She smacked her own forehead. "I've got to get out of the state!"

"Well, you're okay there, Heidi," I told her, "because by tomorrow at this time we'll be in New York—the Big Apple or whatever."

"Tomorrow?" She looked at me, and her eyes started filling up. Heidi misses a lot of meals with her family, so she's not always up on current events. "Tomorrow? What am I going to do with myself in New York for *two weeks*? Listen, I'm not hanging out with you and Luke. That's out. And what about . . ."

"Thor Desmond?" I said. "Look at it this way. Maybe Melissa made him up. Maybe she figured you weren't going to be able to stay at her house anyway, and she was just trying to make you feel worse about going to New York. Besides, you both read too many of those romance books."

"Melissa would never—"

"The light's changed, Heidi. You can go now," I said, "real slow."

We made it home a full five minutes before Mom did. Which is luckier than some of us deserved.

We parked in the exact same spot, and when we were out on the drive, solid blacktop felt good under our feet. Luke staggered.

"Look on the bright side," I said. "Maybe you'll meet a guy in New York."

"Be real," Heidi said, and went to her room.

Two

Mom had cleaned out the refrigerator, so all of us but Al went out to dinner that night.

Al was going to New York with us in the morning, but Luke couldn't explain it to her. He gave her a double order of Burger Bits to keep her busy. But she followed us all the way to the door. Then she sat down with one paw up, wanting to shake, as we left. Every time we leave the house, Al thinks maybe we're never coming back.

Heidi appeared at the last minute, pale and wearing a skirt. Ever since we'd taken our spin in the Taurus, she'd been hiding in her room with the phone turned off.

We knew where we'd be eating—Fang Castle. It's Dad's favorite, and he thinks it's great family entertainment. The theme's year-round Halloween. Guys in Dracula capes park the car, and you walk across a drawbridge over a bogus moat. The place is a former K mart, with Styrofoam turrets and gas torches. The host stands in an upright coffin, and when you shake his hand, it comes off.

The main restaurant is the Stephen King Memorial Room, but we like the Jason Lounge. It's pretty dark, with a lot of hockey masks. The hallway down to the Exorcist Juice Bar is called Elm Street.

We stumbled around in the gloom until we were all sitting down, squinting at menus. A guy came up. "Hi, I'm your waiter, Michael Myers."

"Gross me out," Heidi said.

"Hey, does the Munchkin need a booster chair?" Mike asked, which made Luke sit up straight and as tall as he gets.

The food's regular, though the salad bar's laid out on that table where Frankenstein's monster came to life. Luke and I act a little scared to please Dad. It's a tradition, though we keep forgetting.

Then we were waiting for our food, and Luke was fiddling with a rubber spider, which they provide. He was tucked in next to Dad, and Dad's arm around Luke's shoulder looked huge. Mom and Dad always thought Luke was pretty cute and smart for his age—gifted, in fact. Sometimes I wondered if they noticed he was somewhat strange. They could see he could take Fang Castle or leave it. He was that way about scary movies too. We'd rent a Poltergeist film, and Mom would have her hand over her eyes, and Dad's knuckles would get real white on his chair arm. And Luke would be in Dad's lap, nodding off to sleep. He always knew the difference between real and fake, and I never saw him scared, except maybe when Heidi was driving.

"This New York trip's going to be great," Dad said.

"Hey, you kids are growing up fast. One of these days you won't even want to travel with the whole family."

Heidi sighed.

"Luke, do you think you're going to like New York?" Dad gave him a squeeze. He really wanted us to get enthusiastic about this trip.

"It'll probably be okay," Luke said. "It's an old city." He looked around the Jason Lounge, which had trick cobwebs hanging down from beaverboard beams. "I mean really old, not like this."

Luke always liked old things better than new, which is unusual for a kid his age. Everything in El Rancho Bravo where we live is exactly eleven years old, so we're short on history around here. I wondered if he might overdose on all the history in New York. I tend to worry about things, and I was a little worried about New York anyway. We were going to fly, and I'm a Californian. Being three thousand miles from our car was a hard concept for me.

"How are we going to get around in New York?" I asked Mom. She was looking specially good tonight. She really lit up the Jason Lounge.

"Oh," she said, "well, I guess everything's . . . close."

The Schultzes are closer, Heidi said, but she spoke silently. I read her lips. The fight had really gone out of her.

"And we're not going to be ordinary tourists," Dad said. "We're going to live like real New Yorkers. I'll be going to work. Your mom has a friend living there. We'll be staying in a neighborhood. It'll be the experience of our lives." He's got quite a reach, and he reached across the table to ruffle up my hair. "Right, Chad?"

"Right, Dad." And he was. Our trip to New York would definitely turn out to be the experience of a lifetime. Several lifetimes.

Mike brought our meals. Most of us had hamburgers and cottage fries, listed on the menu as Dead Meat and Tombstones.

When we got home from Fang Castle, Al yapped around our feet and wanted us to sit down so she could get up in our laps. Heidi was already in her room. Mom took me aside.

"Chad, I have a feeling I'm going to have my hands full with Heidi in New York. I'm counting on you to keep an eye on Luke. He's imaginative, you know, and intelligent. But he's still a little boy."

"I try to remember that, Mom. I'll watch him." I started up the stairs.

"And another thing, Chad. Do you have any idea why Heidi isn't making a last-ditch effort to stay behind with the Schultzes?"

"Do you want the truth, Mom?"

She thought about that. But she just gave me a kiss good-night and said, "I guess not."

I was almost too keyed up to sleep. My big canvas carryall was by my bed, full. I'd packed a basketball, but Dad said not to bother. He's about six four and played center at UCLA before his knees gave him trouble. He and Luke and I still get out in the evenings and shoot some hoops on the driveway. I'm a foot taller than Luke. Dad's a foot taller than I am, so we're not exactly the Celtics, but we enjoy it. But Dad said they didn't have driveways in New York.

Before I even knew I was asleep, my snow dream came back. It was different this time, scarier. I could hear it, first a whistling of the wind through the cracks of an old house. Then a roar, louder than a jet. I was in a room dim as a cave, and the snow was pounding at the window, whirling against it with a force like fists. It was an old window, with panes. I knew the wind would blow them out. Before it happened, I could tell the window would explode. The glass would fly all over the room like crystal knives. And the snow would follow, and find me.

Over the roar I heard birds. Somewhere there were birds, chattering. They'd tried to escape the wind and the snow and were in this place with me. But we were doomed. The windowpanes cracked then, all together like a firing squad. I threw an arm over my eyes.

And sat up in bed. I was still in my own room at home. It took a minute for me to know that this was real and the dream wasn't. I saw all the familiar shapes in the room, and the door to the hall. It was open.

I was still scared and trying to deal with it when a shadow went down the hall past my door. A small shadow, but not as small as Al. The hair on the back of my head lifted, even though I knew it was Luke.

He's a sleepwalker. You hear little footsteps somewhere in the house. Then somebody has to get up and lead Luke back to bed. I'm not even sure it's sleepwalking, but he wanders around a lot at night. His mind's always going a mile a minute, and he really has to wear himself out to get any sleep at all. I threw back my sheet and got up. I wasn't that anxious to get back to Nuclear Winter again, or whatever that dream was.

When a dream scares you, you don't go down to your little brother's room for company. It doesn't work that way. I strolled down the hall. When I got to Luke's door, I dropped in, just to check on him. He was this small mound in the bed. I settled down on the end of it.

"Luke? You were walking in your sleep again."

"Was I?" he said, far off. I could see the tip of his nose above the sheet and his head burrowed deep in the pillow because he still sleeps with a night-light. The way my dreams were going, I thought I might go back to a night-light myself.

"You dream much, Luke?"

"A lot," came this muffled voice.

"What do you dream about?" I said, keeping it casual.

"Until lately, tomatoes."

Tomatoes? "You dream about tomatoes?"

"Fields and fields of tomatoes," he said, "as far as you can see."

"How come?"

His sheet seemed to shrug. "That's all that was around here before they built El Rancho Bravo. This territory was just fields and fields of tomatoes, with maybe a line of olive trees for a windbreak."

Weird. "Do you always dream about the past, Luke?"

"Doesn't everybody?" He was slipping away now. His voice was farther off.

"Dreaming about tomato fields sounds pretty boring," I said.

"It is," he said, nodding in his pillow. "I'll probably dream better in New York. I already am. Good night, Chad."

I can take a hint. When I stood up, something snorted and then sighed under the bed—Al, who sleeps there. Luke's breathing was steady now, rising and falling. He was dead to the world.

When I got to the door, he spoke again, from the depths of a dream.

"Better put another blanket on, Chad. It's snowing up a storm."

The next day we went to New York.

Three

Dad's firm had gone through an agency to rent us a place on East Seventy-third Street. Central Park was right down there at the end of the block. It was a house, and we had part of it. There were high-rises on the corner, and you could tell that Seventy-third Street was always in shadow. It was like the toy village under a Christmas tree, everything quaint and chocolate-colored. Flaky old stone steps went up to a tall front door.

None of us but Dad had ever been to New York, and I'd never seen anything like this before. The house wasn't spooky. It was just old, and narrow like the street. It went up five stories if you count the attic. You could see clean curtains on the paned windows of the main floor and the two floors above it. I don't think I looked higher than that. Later I tried to remember and couldn't.

We'd taken a couple of cabs in from JFK, so we'd had our first view of the Manhattan skyline against the setting sun. Fire above and evening below with a billion twinkling lights. Even Heidi looked. When the cabs pulled away, Al was out on the pavement, stunned. She'd just traveled on a transcontinental flight as checked baggage. Now she was staring down between

her paws at the first sidewalk she'd ever seen. We
started relaying the bags up the front steps, which Dad
called a stoop. He had the key, and when he turned it in
the lock, it set off a burglar alarm. It was a real screech
you could hear out at sea. But it didn't alert the cops or
the neighbors. Dad was inside, feeling the wall for the
cutoff. When he found it, we stood there deaf in the
sudden silence.

Then we started exploring. Down one flight was the
kitchen, tucked in under the stoop, and behind it an
open-plan dining area. It was all top of the line, even if
it was in the basement. The main floor was even better.
There were two big rooms, back and front, a living
room and a family room, if you can picture a family
room without sliders onto a deck.

An alcove room at the back was fitted out as a total
home entertainment center: TV with oversized screen,
laser-disc player, an Atari ST with a full library of In-
focomics and Nintendo—everything state of the art.
Luke glanced in there, but he wasn't interested. He's
never watched much TV. He hadn't even liked *Sesame
Street.* He said Big Bird was made out of synthetic mate-
rials.

Both the big rooms looked like photographs from
Architectural Digest. They'd kept the two old marble
fireplaces, but the pictures over them were modern art
in chrome frames. The pictures themselves were just a
couple of dots. It was all impressive: thick glass tables

and track lighting; oyster-white carpeting wall-to-wall throughout.

But out in the hall it was different. This big old carved-wood stairway went up the middle of the house around a square opening three stories high. Here at the bottom in the front hall was a big bird cage with curly brass bars. The staircase went up around it.

"Would you look at this?" Mom said. The big bird cage had double doors. Inside was a little chair with a telephone on a table. It looked like the world's most expensive antique telephone booth.

"Honey," Mom said to Dad, "what is the rent on this place costing the company?"

"Three thousand a week," Dad said.

Mom sank into a chair just inside the front living room. "Kids, listen, don't break anything. Don't touch anything. Where's the dog?"

Actually Al caused quite a problem. In New York you can't just let a dog out to do its business and wait for it to come back and scratch on the sliders to come in. You have to take the dog for a walk. It gets worse.

After we'd settled in and done a little unpacking, we all took Al out. You not only have to walk them, you have to clean up after them. It's New York law. Dad brought along some Baggies and a spatula. I gave Al her first lesson in walking on a leash and steered her into gutters. Dad and Luke came along behind as cleanup crew.

We explored over across Park Avenue as far as Lexington to see if there were supermarkets. There weren't, not as we know them. But little stores had fruit piled out in the open. It looked Third World to me. Heidi kept dropping back, looking for a Benetton. But Luke ambled along in his thoughtful way, swinging a spatula.

"Do you realize we've never taken a walk before?" Dad said, "on sidewalks? as a family? Is this great or what?"

We kind of stood out here. We were the only pedestrians with good tans, and we were sure tidier than most. All ten of our snow-white running shoes glowed in the dark. Mom was clinging to Dad because a lot of people wandering around at night looked like they were out on bail.

"You can really feel the pulse of the city," Dad said.

We bought some groceries by shopping around, but you had to buy what they had. Then it was funny not being able to heave all your sacks into the trunk of the Taurus.

Mom and Dad took the second-floor front bedroom. Heidi took the back one on their floor. Luke and I were on the third floor. I offered to share my room with him, but he went on down the dark hall to a room at the back, pretty far from all of us.

I had a good room, like a four-star hotel. Jet lag zapped me, and I fell into bed. But as soon as I turned off my light, I was wide awake. I kept hearing little feet out in the hall, four little feet. It was Al, up and down the hallway, completely stumped by this new environment. She wasn't any too bright even at home.

The house had central air-conditioning, so the windows were sealed. But you could hear traffic down on Seventy-third Street. Car burglar alarms sounded off all over the city. You always hear things the first night in a new place, and you think you stay awake longer than you do.

I was in dreamland then, looking around for snow. But there wasn't any. I was in this bed in this room, and I'd have thought I was still awake except for the voices. They were floating in from the hall. No, they were a little farther off than that, but out there somewhere. Voices after midnight. They were talking to each other, and I could hear.

"*Soon now,*" he said. "*Any moment now. You must not give up hope.*"

Who was he? I didn't know, but in a way it seemed to be a voice I'd been hearing all my life.

"*Take my hands,*" she said. "*They're blue with cold.*"

She? I could feel the tension all over the house. I even knew I was there in bed, my back starting to arch, my hands clenching up into fists.

"*When will we be free of this prison?*" she said in a broken voice.

"*Soon,*" he said, but he didn't believe it. I guess everybody has dreams where nothing makes sense, but you can follow what's happening.

I was trying to wake up, but I couldn't breathe. I was

locked in, and something was shutting off my wind. A claw on my throat. My eyes popped open, and there was gray morning light across my ceiling, what I could see of it.

Al was all over me, planted right across my neck. It was like being strangled by a thick, fur-bearing sausage. She wasn't asleep because she wasn't snoring. She never jumped up on my bed. She always slept under Luke's. I reached up to pull her off by the collar, but one of her sharp claws dug into my throat. I managed to slip out from under her, but then she dug right into my pillow, and whimpered. She was scared.

Even when I was out of bed, she stayed hunched up against the headboard, her eyes bulging farther out than usual. The room was dark and boxy, just shapes. A breeze stirred the curtains at the open window. I went over and looked down on Seventy-third Street.

They must have parking regulations because all the cars were gone. The neighborhood was still asleep. But there was a surprising sight down there, a horse-drawn cart. A horse in a straw hat with ear holes, and this cart with big old polished milk cans. There were a lot of horse droppings on the street too. The morning air was none too fresh.

A man in a leather apron was tipping milk out of a can into an open pail. He carried it up the steps of the house next door. When I leaned out the window to watch him, I saw a girl sitting on our stoop right below me.

Heidi? Heidi sitting outside before dawn in her bathrobe or something, clutching her knees, there on the top step? I couldn't really see. I nearly yelled down to her, but didn't. The milkman nodded her way, touching his cap.

But I was so tired I could have fallen out the window. I dropped back into bed, and Al made room for me, glad to have me back. When I woke up again, it was brighter morning. Al was down at the end of my bed, burrowed. I could feel her snores on my toes.

And that business with the milkman had to be a dream. How could I have leaned out a sealed window? What happened to central air-conditioning?

Four

Dad was down for breakfast in a sharp new summer suit he'd be wearing to the New York office. Mom was still upstairs in the bird cage on the phone with her college friend, Mary Lou, who lives in New York. They hadn't seen each other since college. Even Heidi was at the breakfast bar with us. She was quiet this morning and kind of huddled near Dad. It's been several years since I'd seen Heidi at breakfast. Luke was there, but he's an early riser.

Dad was just asking us about our plans for our first day in the city when Mom came in, looking like Linda Evans even this early.

"Guess what," she said. "Mary Lou wants Heidi and me to meet her for shopping and a late lunch."

Heidi sighed. She and Melissa have a rule about never going into a store with their mothers. I'm not sure what it means.

"And Mary Lou's daughter is just home from boarding school and dying to meet you, Heidi. Jocelyn's just your age."

The idea of a New York girl named Jocelyn who goes to boarding school even scared me, so you can imagine what it did to Heidi.

"It'll be wonderful to see Mary Lou again," Mom said.

"And it'll be nice for you to have a friend your age, Heidi. You won't miss Melissa so much."

Heidi's eyes misted over like she was going to bust out crying. I expected her to say she'd be staying home all day by herself. But she didn't. Something was bothering her, even apart from having breakfast with us.

Giving Mom a private wink, I said, "It's cool, Heidi. You can spend the day with me and Luke. We're going to scout out Central Park—walk ten or twelve miles and really get the feel of the place."

"No way," she said automatically.

So that's how she happened to spend the day with Mom and Jocelyn's mom and Jocelyn. I noticed she wasn't about to hang around in this house by herself. Sometimes I can read Heidi.

Mom wasn't thrilled about me and Luke going to Central Park on our own. But Dad said it would help us get our bearings. So we went, taking Al with us. She was jumpy. Yesterday she'd flown three thousand air miles in a 747, caged. Now she was afraid of the traffic. We dragged her halfway to the park before she'd walk right. Then I had to carry her across Fifth Avenue and plop her down in the first grass we saw.

At the Seventy-second Street entrance there was a big framed map of the park, but Luke strolled right past it. "You're going to like this park, Chad," he said, like a tour guide.

We started in under big trees. I'd just got Al waddling right when Luke veered off and walked straight into a hedge, face first. He didn't even put up his hands to shield himself. He barged in between two park benches, and the people sitting there really noticed. When I dragged him back, he had twigs in his T-shirt and leaves in his hair.

"There used to be a bridle path there," he said.

I could have used another leash.

"Let's hang a right down there," he said. "It'll lead to Conservatory Water. There'll probably be some kids sailing little boats on it."

We walked on and, you guessed it, we came to a pond with small kids sailing model boats.

"Tell me, Luke. How did you know this was here?"

"Always has been." He moved on ahead to see the toy boats. We walked around the water and found a tunnel under a drive. It led to the Loeb Boathouse. The day was heating up, so we tied Al to a bike rack in the shade and went inside for a couple of colas. You could sit out on a good deck overlooking a bigger lake with real boats and the skyline of the city beyond it.

"It's better in the winter," Luke said, fooling with his soda straw. "They skated here before the ice rink was built. With bonfires on the shore. All the hot chocolate you could drink."

"I guess you probably saw an old picture of it in the winter, in a book."

"I may have," he said.

He was getting restless and ready to go before he finished his drink. But he wasn't bored. Far from it. I could see he was overstimulated. Most young kids don't care about anything unless it's a zoo or a playground. But Luke wasn't most young kids.

We went on to find a fake castle, the Belvedere, which he knew before it came in sight. He really had a feel for this park. When we got to the Great Lawn, which was full of people kicking around soccer balls, I let Al off the leash and watched her and Luke bound on ahead. This was more open country than I'd expected to find in New York. But it didn't seem to come as any surprise to Luke.

We were moving up on the back of the Metropolitan Museum of Art. Behind it on a little knoll was a stone pillar about seventy feet high. It was carved all over and came to a point, Egyptian.

"Cleopatra's Needle," Luke said when I caught up with him. Since we were seeing the sights that day, I thought we might have a closer look at it. The thing was really impressive. But Luke reined in Al and held his ground.

"What's wrong? Don't you want to see it?"

He was digging in and not moving. "I'm hot," he said, whiny. "It's too hot."

It was fairly hot, but there was a breeze. Still, sweat popped out on his forehead under the flop of his blond hair. We stood there, me trying to figure out what was going on, as usual. I wished I'd made him wear his cap.

"It's an obelisk," he said, "for the Temple of the Sun at Heliopolis. You can feel the heat from here—Egypt."

"It goes way back, I guess."

"Too far," Luke said. "It was venerable when Moses enjoyed the favor of the Egyptian court as the son of Pharaoh's daughter."

"Say what?"

"It's old. I've never been close to anything this old. I better be careful."

So we gave Cleopatra's Needle a wide berth, to please Luke. Then we were up north above the Reservoir. It smelled almost like country. We were up on rough park land, and Luke was in the lead. Al's tongue was beginning to drag grass.

"It's around here someplace." Then Luke nodded at a run-down old stone building like a fort, up on a cliff. "It's a powder house from the War of 1812. It's where they stored their ammo."

"Is it too old to go near?" I was still kind of humoring him.

"It's okay. I was just checking to see if it was still here." Cool, he picked up a stick and threw it for Al. We turned around, retracing our steps. Al doesn't retrieve. When she found the stick, she got tangled up and fell over it.

It was afternoon by then. We were climbing through pretty rugged territory, not even like a park now, not even paths. The leaves made patterns where we stepped. The city sounds seemed miles away. Luke stopped in a little clearing.

"Right in through here the army retreated after we lost the Battle of Long Island."

"War of 1812?"

"Revolutionary. If you dug down, you could probably find some of their old earthworks. I bet you could."

Then Al spoke. She rarely does, and this was just a low growl.

"All this nature's getting to her," I said. "She's going to turn into a wild killer-pug."

"No," Luke said, quieter than the breeze. "We're not alone. She knows."

I looked around and didn't see anybody. Just hazy sun playing through dusty leaves. It shouldn't have been creepy, but it was. Luke pointed down into a ravine past some big rocks.

There were some guys down there, stumbling along a hidden path. They must have been in show business because they were in these ragged old uniforms, the kind with big lapels and a lot of tarnished buttons. They were carrying historic muskets—authentic. They even had powder horns slung on leather straps. They were moving along the path without making any noise. Some of them were bandaged up, with red for the blood, and brown blood and gray bandages for the older wounds. They went single file and a few in groups, helping each other. One or two looked back over their shoulders. They all needed shaves.

After they were gone, we kept watching. There was nothing down there now but wildflowers. Maybe a squirrel. We walked on, up a rise, down a dip. Then amazingly, we stepped through a screen of trees onto the sidewalk of Fifth Avenue, at the corner of 103rd Street. A guy in a paper cap was selling hot dogs and fried onions off a portable grill. We had lunch.

It smelled better than it was. It was mostly bun. We stood by a trash can, feeding Al leftovers. "Listen, Luke, who do you suppose those dressed-up guys were down in those rocks?"

He looked up and made a little mouth. "I was pretty sure you saw them."

"Of course I saw them. How could I miss? *Al* saw them."

Luke was looking up at me, nodding.

"But it was different with you, Luke. I think you knew they were going to be there—ahead of time."

Since he was wearing shorts, the mosquitoes up in the woods had gotten to his legs. He reached down a Nike sock and scratched. "I kind of knew," he said softly. "I figured."

He had me worried now, which I don't like to be. A question came to me. "Listen, Luke, you haven't been dreaming about this park, have you? And old soldiers and battles back in history?"

He cocked his head and tried to scratch his ear with his shoulder. "It's possible. Last night I sure didn't dream about boring old tomato fields like we have back home. My dreams were so busy last night I couldn't keep up with them. There's so much history here in New York, it's coming out of our ears."

A light changed, and a flood of cabs surged down Fifth Avenue beside us. "Luke, you're not trying to say that those guys down in the gully dressed up like old-time soldiers really were from . . . old times. Don't give me that."

"Okay," he said.

"I'm serious, Luke. People can't see from one time to another, like they're looking over a fence. History's in the library. It's all filed away."

He squashed his paper napkin into a ball and lobbed it into the trash can. "I wouldn't bet on it, Chad. Everything that ever happened is still going on, inside us."

"Like parallel universes or something?"

"Something," Luke said.

"But how do you get in touch with all this?"

"We both can."

"Not me," I said. "Count me out." I was fourteen. Reality was hard enough for me.

"Remember the prospector's cabin on the back of the witchwoman's property?" he said.

"What about it?"

"You saw that. And it isn't here *now*. It was there *then*, in 1849. The witchwoman probably doesn't even know about it. I bet that cabin fell down before she was born. But we saw it. You and me, Chad."

"No way," I said, but my mouth was really dry. I was beginning to forget I was the older brother. "Okay," I said, keeping it light. "How come we have this great power and other people don't? Why us?"

He turned up a pair of grubby palms. "I guess anybody could have it. But most people spend too much of their time thinking about now and themselves. And then there's TV. I never watched much, so I've kept pretty alert."

He looked up at me, serious, and blinked once. "And I think maybe we have a special job to do. I think maybe there's some unfinished business for us to take care of. I think it's around here someplace if we can find it."

He gazed around, and I had no idea what he was seeing. But I had this urge—just a slight one—to grab him by his ankles and dangle him over the trash can until he started talking sense. But I'm cool.

"Another thing, Luke. Where do you get words like *obelisk* and *venerable*? You were throwing them around a while ago."

"Oh, well," he said, "they're in the dictionary, alphabetized."

So I gave up, and we started home, down Fifth Avenue like regular pedestrians. Farther along I noticed that Luke had put two Baggies on his hands and was wearing them like gloves. It was a typical kid thing to do, and he seemed just like a normal kid, and why not leave it that way?

We had our own key, so when we got back to Seventy-third Street, we bounded up the stoop and let ourselves in. The burglar alarm was already shut off. But I didn't think much about it. While Luke was getting the leash off Al, I headed on upstairs.

Somebody was coming down. We met on that first landing behind the bird cage. It seemed to be a girl. She stopped, and I jumped a foot. I'd never seen her before. I'd never seen anybody like her. She was wearing a loose black-and-white striped Guess? top and baggy shorts over a skinny figure. And very big socks over Beastie Boy–type shoes. She was completely black and white, even her face. Snow-white makeup with black lips and hair slicked back smooth. She was a ripple or two ahead of New Wave.

"Oh, hi," she said. "You must be one of the brothers. Are you the weird one or the pest?"

By now Luke had caught up and was peering around me at her.

"Ah . . . I'd be the pest," I said. "This is the—this is Luke."

Her gaze skimmed just over my head.

"And you'd be Jocelyn?" I said, taking a stab at it.

She nodded, just a little. "Like welcome to New York. When my mother said we were entertaining a college friend of hers and the daughter, I thought about having one of my migraines. But honestly, your sister's got a lot of potential."

I could tell that Luke was fascinated. We both were. We'd never seen anybody who could talk without moving her jaw.

"Yeah, we're real proud of Heidi," I said.

"I'd never met anybody who went to public school before," Jocelyn said. "It's been a real cultural exchange."

"Say, Jocelyn," I said, "have you seen anything of our mom?" I was feeling trapped here on the landing. I'm not that sure of myself around girls. And this one made me feel like a Pee-wee Herman doll. I was beginning to wonder if I was wearing a bow tie.

Jocelyn sighed. "Our mothers are both down in your dining area, drinking iced tea and talking about their college days, and talking and talking."

"Is your mom as pretty as our mom?" Luke piped up from behind me.

"Pretty?" Jocelyn's black brows rose. "How can they be pretty? They're thirty-eight."

Suddenly Heidi appeared out of the second-floor hall. It was a half-new Heidi. She still had a lot of blond hair, California style. But she'd painted over her tan with dead-white makeup, and she had Jocelyn lips—spider black. She was wearing a new outfit, too, several shades of black. Jocelyn had been giving her makeup tips, and they'd had a busy day in the stores, which works for Heidi. Her favorite sweatshirt reads SHOP TILL YOU DROP.

"Wow, Heidi, you know who should see you now?" I said. "Melissa."

"Who?" Heidi said, so I saw right there she was settling into New York.

Five

Evening comes quicker in a New York town house. The sun dips behind high-rises, and everything goes gray. Jocelyn and her mom had been gone an hour when Luke and I started upstairs again. As we got to the second floor, we heard hissing. It was either a snake, escaping gas, or Heidi.

"Pssst," she said from her door down the hall. "Chad? Luke? Come in here a minute, okay?"

All our bedrooms were pretty much the same, everything new like a model home. But Heidi had brought her whole library from California, which explained why her luggage had weighed a ton. Her room was lined with the complete paperback series of Pep Squadders in Love. She also had all sixty volumes, numbered, in the Meaningful Moments at Honeybrook High series. She was a romance fan and couldn't part with them. The only other thing she'd brought from home was her poster of Maverick from *Top Gun*.

"What's happening, Heidi?"

But Luke saw it before she pointed. Something was on her bedside table. Closer, we saw it was a tight little bouquet of dried flowers: small, rolled-up yellowish flowers that could have been crocuses. They were tied up with leaves in lacy paper by a long ribbon. The thing looked out of place here, especially next to Maverick.

"Look closer," Heidi said, almost in a whisper.

The long ribbon had a message glued on it in old gold paper letters:

WITH RESPECTFUL AFFECTION
T.D.

T.D.? My mind was gunning in neutral, like it does a lot. Luke was looking and rubbing his chin.

"Let's assume this isn't one of your little pranks," Heidi said in a calm and reasonable voice that reminded me of Mom. "When did it get here? And how? Federal Express? Teleflorist? Talk to me, Chad." The evening glowed on her new all-white face.

"Hey, Heidi, Luke and I haven't been delivering anything. We've been in the park all day."

Her black lips pursed, but she couldn't hold herself in any longer. "Look who it's from! T.D.—Thor Desmond. Thank heaven I left this address with Melissa!"

Heidi cut loose, reaching for the ceiling and swiveling around in a pep squadders' victory dance. "Thor Desmond!" she said, going wild. "He's probably coming to New York! We'll probably go out here! A buggy ride in the park! The Rainbow Room! What'll I wear?"

We crept away then while she was still on a roll.

"Thor Desmond?" I said to Luke as we ambled down the hall.

"No way," he said, starting up the stairs.

In bed that night, just as I was drifting off, I heard something. Wind, gale-force wind, whipped around the house, crying at the windows, trying to get in. I thought I was back in my blizzard dream, but there was something different. I heard something at the heart of the house, the sound of clanking metal. And it sure wasn't a Honda Gyro. I almost knew what it was, but not quite. Maybe I wasn't even asleep.

The voices were back, in my head and in these rooms around me. I'd known they would be. I'd waited all day to hear them without realizing, his voice and hers. I'd heard them last night. Now they were—not nearer, but clearer.

"Think of sky," he said. *"The park. Think of the park, on the warmest day of summer. Think of running in the sunlight over the meadows."*

I held my breath in the dream, in real life, because she was going to answer him. This girl. Not Heidi, not Jocelyn. Not any girl I'd ever known.

"Oh no, not that," she said. *"It's a cruel thought."*

Why? I tried to yell, the way you try in dreams and can't.

"I must sleep soon," she said, and there was something really final in her voice, like sleeping was something she couldn't put off any longer.

"No," he said, and his voice cracked. *"You must not sleep. I can't let you do that. No!"* He slapped her, and it was loud enough to wake me. He'd slapped her hard in the face so she wouldn't sleep. But that's all I knew. I didn't even know who they were, quite.

I was awake, wringing wet and freezing. Even the sheets were brittle with the cold. But the room was normal, so why was I too scared to move? A ghost of a sound came from somewhere outside the bedroom door. I'd have let it pass, but I thought of Luke. It was just daylight, and I could half see. I was out of bed, and when I got out in the hall, I panicked.

Down at the other end Luke's door was open. Morning light came in his back windows. I could see the foot of his empty bed. He was sleepwalking again, or whatever he did. All I could think of was that sheer drop in the middle of the stairs.

In a quick sprint I was there. I don't know why I was so sure he'd fallen down the stairwell. But I grabbed the railing and looked all the way down to the front hall. I could see down there too, barely.

He wasn't there, but I didn't like any of this. I'm not crazy about heights anyway, and down at the bottom of the stairs was that big brass bird-cage phone booth. I hadn't noticed before, but it had a fancy metal dome on top. At the center was a spike like the top of a flagpole, gleaming in brass and sharp enough to go right through you.

I couldn't even look at it. I glanced over at the narrow

staircase that led on up to the top of the house from our floor. It was almost a secret passage, all boxed in with a padlocked door up a couple of steps.

Luke was standing there. I wouldn't have noticed because of the shadows, but I saw the pale color of his hair and the white of his Jockey shorts, which is all he sleeps in. He was up there on the step, like a statue in front of the locked door. He was facing me, hoping I wouldn't see him.

Now, that made me mad, but I walked around to him. The big open stairway led down right beside us, so I was careful. "Luke, are you awake?"

"It's almost morning," he said, like an excuse.

"Were you trying to hide from me?"

He moved his head, either up and down or sideways. Kidlike. But then he said, "I can't always wait for you, Chad. I have a lot to do."

"You mean you want to go upstairs, to the attic or wherever?"

"I need to check this place out," he said. "To find out where the voices are coming from."

"What do you mean, Luke? Like voices in your dreams?"

"Not really dreams," he said, faintly.

"Do they talk to you?"

He shook his head, sure about it. "They talk to each other. I don't think they know I'm there."

"How are you going to get upstairs? Do you have a key to the padlock?"

He turned on the narrow step and pulled on the padlock. It slipped open. He looked back at me, not blinking. "I can unlock the past," he said. "You know that."

I didn't know what I knew. I knew we were awake. He pushed me back so he could swing the door open. I was stepping back, careful not to fall down the big stairs, not wanting any of this to be happening.

The door sobbed on its hinges, and we were at the foot of another flight of stairs. Light filtered through cobwebs from windows up there. Luke started climbing, a step at a time. And I had to go with him.

"We're probably not supposed to be up here," I said. "We didn't rent this part."

Now we were up in a hallway, narrower. The ceiling was low, and it was hot as an oven even at dawn. Luke raised dust with every step as he padded from room to room, barefoot, checking it all out. It was all in bad shape, and seemed empty. I sure hoped so.

It was like a different house up here, trapped in time. In every little boxy room wallpaper hung down in strips, old wallpaper with colorless morning glories. In a couple of rooms the ceilings had come down. The floors were dunes of powdered plaster. I'll tell you what it made me think of. It felt like everybody had moved out a long time ago, just walked out of this house and never even wanted to look back.

They'd taken most of the furniture. There were only a couple of beds, knocked apart and leaning webbed to the wall. You couldn't see anything out of the windows. Still, there was more light up here. Day came here first. I hung around in the hall, waiting for Luke. The air was thick with dust particles like trillions of little worlds.

"Who do you suppose lived up here?"

When he came out of one of the rooms, his face looked blurred. I wondered if he was coming down with something.

"Girls," he said.

Girls?

"Girls with big aprons."

"Like maids?"

"Like that. But I can't really see them. It's just a memory of them. They're already gone. Been gone for years."

Suits me, I thought. I was ready to go myself. But Luke said, "Let's try the attic." So we had another flight to climb to the top of the house. The door at the head of the stairs was flimsy, not even locked.

I didn't see anything at first, except for the dormer windows. They were in the slanting roof, looking down on Seventy-third Street. We seemed to have the same feeling. We were being watched.

Believe me, I wouldn't have hung around to find out, but Luke held his ground, looking all around the attic, really interested. He pointed to a chimney that came up through the house. Behind it was an eye. This big, staring eye, brown. Luke went over to it. By now I saw it was glass, the eye of a hobby horse wedged in behind the chimney. It was this fake pony on wooden rockers and really moth eaten. It was fading away, blending in. A lot of it had disintegrated.

"Just a toy," I said.

"A toy, too late," Luke said. "Nobody's played with it for years." He thought of something. "Try the window."

Three of them were spaced across the front of the house. The one we tried was nailed shut with tenpenny nails. But Luke went to work, rubbing a clean spot. He looked down to the street, and his eyes widened. Then he looked up over the roofs of the houses on the uptown side of the street.

"What, Luke? I'm getting tired of this."

But he just brought up his little bird-bone shoulders and walked away in his underpants like he couldn't be bothered to explain anything. When I looked out, I didn't think I saw anything in particular. Down on Seventy-third Street some cars were going by. They were big square black ones, sort of like hearses.

Across the street were the dormer windows of the houses over there. I saw a woman in one of them. She was bustling around an attic bedroom, getting ready for work. She was young, with funny, straight, cut-off red hair. I watched her pull on an odd hat. It was like a helmet, coming down low on her forehead. She checked herself in a mirror and swayed out of the room on high heels. That was all. I looked up above the houses and saw the steel skeleton of a tall building under construction. It was northeast of us, standing alone in the sky. The morning sun made its girders bright. Behind me one of the attic steps creaked. I whirled around because we weren't alone.

Heidi was standing at the top of the stairs in her shorty pajamas. Her early-morning hair was a big blond halo around her head. She hadn't put on any makeup yet, so she was still tan, and her eyes were just dots.

"You two." She sighed. "I woke up and heard these footsteps way up here someplace. Might have known."

But she seemed interested in the attic, even though it was a wreck. She even spotted something Luke and I had overlooked. It was a trunk under the eaves, gray with dust. You could tell from here it wasn't locked. The leather straps were falling apart. Heidi went right for it. She dropped to her knees and reached for the lid.

"Easy, Heidi," I said, and not just to scare her. There was something about this whole attic I could do without. And I didn't feel great about an old trunk up here. I had this sudden idea it might have body parts in it, sawed up into handy lengths.

Luke was there when she propped the lid back. Layers of tissue paper were on top. When Heidi touched them, her nails went right through. Now she was fingering the corner of something down in the trunk. It was lace, possibly a dress.

"Be sure nobody's wearing it, Heidi," I said near her ear.

But she was unfolding it out of the powdery paper. It

was a complicated dress with ribbons and lace, ivory colored with age. It was old as the hills.

"Vintage," Heidi whispered, and she couldn't take her eyes off it. She held it up against herself, being careful with it. Then she did a little thing with her head, just a quick shake. It's what girls do when they're imagining. She was imagining herself in this dress, even though it sure wasn't any of her images. She was being the kind of girl for a dress like this. Sometimes I can read Heidi.

Then she remembered we were there. She folded the dress back into the trunk and pulled the shreds of paper over it and dropped the lid down. When she got up and started for the stairs, she moved in a different way, more graceful. Luke and I watched her going down the stairs until her uncombed head disappeared from view.

By now Luke was really restless. He was practically doing a dance. "Come on," he said. "It's getting late. Mom and Dad will be awake any minute. Let's go. We can be out of the house and back again before anybody notices."

He was at the stairs already. I didn't bother to ask him what our hurry was or where we were going. I wanted out. This whole house, the living part down below and the dead part up here, was getting on my nerves.

In five minutes we were dressed and down at the front door. Al was ahead of us. Her leash hung on the knob, and she was staring straight at her Baggies box, wanting to go out.

"Do we take Al?"

Luke smiled like this would be a good reason for being out of the house. On the stoop it was a bright early summer morning. It looked good to me, the brick and the brownstone, the glossy green of the trees, the colors of the cars.

Luke led me by the hand around the corner where Soup Burg is and up Madison Avenue. Except for some bus traffic, the street was still waking up. We went past the Whitney Museum of American Art, which Luke didn't bother to notice. At Seventy-sixth Street on the H. L. Purdy Optician corner, he waited for the light to change. No cars were coming, but he stood there, looking up at me. Al waited. Across the street was the Carlyle Hotel, standing alone, an expensive-looking place and fairly old. The light changed. We could walk. Luke didn't.

"I give up. What?"

Then it dawned on me. I looked up at the Carlyle Hotel, and it was a solid structure, not new, standing alone. It wasn't under construction. It wasn't just a steel skeleton with the morning sun hitting its beams. But it was the same building under construction we'd both seen out the attic window not even half an hour ago. I didn't want to know this, and it was true.

Luke and Al crossed. I kept up. A doorman was on

duty, and Luke went right for him. "Could you tell me when this Carlyle Hotel was built?" he said in his high voice.

"Been here quite a while." The doorman looked away up the street, which is the way adults treat kids sometimes. But it didn't matter. On the wall inside the big glass doors was a plaque. We went inside and read it.

THE CARLYLE

THE BEMELMANS BAR

CAFE CARLYLE

Architects: Bien & Price

1929

People went in and out of the hotel behind us. Luke was thinking. I don't know what I was doing. "What does it mean?" I said finally.

"It means we're not far enough back yet. We only got back to 1929 this morning. Maybe 1928. Still, we got back pretty far since we weren't even trying."

"Back?"

"Far enough back in time."

"How far are we going?"

Luke shrugged. "As far as we need to. And you can go, too, Chad."

"Wait a minute."

"Do you hear the voices, his voice and hers?" Luke

spoke so soft I almost didn't hear. "At night in the house, do you hear their voices?"

"What voices?"

"I hear them too. They're back there somewhere in time. I think they want us."

Six

We headed back down Madison Avenue, and all I wanted was to start this day over again in a regular, normal way. Al was getting used to city walks. Her tight little tail bobbed along, and she walked a fairly straight line. But when we stopped for lights, she didn't like the cross traffic and pulled back to sit on our feet.

We made a stop for her off the curb at the Seventy-third Street corner. When I turned back to the trash can, she and Luke wandered on, and that's where she got into big trouble. Luke wasn't watching where they were going, and neither was Al. She walked right in under a Doberman pinscher.

Two Dobermans. It happened fast. When Al looked up, all she saw was Doberman. She shrieked, and they went crazy. They were unusually tall Dobermans, very sleek with well-bred ears and teeth like precision instruments. Al's leash had tangled around the hind legs of this tall dog she was under. Both Dobermans were doing some serious baritone barking, with curled lips.

I came up quick, and Luke and I yanked on the leash. Al came flying back like a fast-pitch softball. She leapt into Luke's arms and began clawing at his shirt.

Somebody was yelling for the police. It was a woman standing by the stoop, braced in bedroom slippers, and she wasn't a lot taller than her dogs. She was jerking their choke chains and screaming for the cops in their ears.

They settled down anyway, and it hit me that she was calling for the police because our pug had attacked her Dobermans.

"This is typical," she yelled. "Where are the cops when you need them? If that animal of yours has hurt my babies, it'll go to the lab to have its head cut off."

Al was still trying to climb Luke's shirt. The Dobermans were just standing around, drooling. She was a really strange lady, small and skinny with orange hair. Under her raincoat she was wearing a nightgown.

"Sorry about that," I said. By now Al was trying to get up on Luke's head. These were the first Dobermans she'd ever seen, and they must be the kind of creatures small dogs have nightmares about.

"And anyway," the old lady said, "what are you two doing on Seventy-third Street? This is a nice, quiet neighborhood."

A paramedic van screamed by, drowning her out.

Al's hind feet were on Luke's shoulder, and her front paws were on his head. She was looking up at me with big pleading eyes.

"We live here," Luke said, pointing across to our house.

"Oh," the old lady said, "renters." Her lipstick matched her hair, and it had worked up into the wrinkles above her mouth. "How long are you here for?"

One of the Dobermans was nuzzling her hand with a big, slobbery mouth.

"Just for a couple of weeks," I said, ". . . ma'am."

She sighed. "People come and go. This used to be a lovely, settled neighborhood. Now it's like the West Side." She reached into her raincoat pocket and took out two doggie candies. "All right, my precious," she said, and popped one into the Doberman's yawning jaw. The other Doberman wheeled on her, to get his candy too. She patted their noses, which I personally wouldn't do with a Doberman.

Al looked down from Luke's head. She was still terrorized, but she heard doggie candy being crunched. The old lady reached for another treat. Both her Dobermans watched her feed it to Al. Luke stood there, gazing up at her, fascinated.

"Why doesn't your animal have a neck?" she asked.

"Because it's a pug," Luke said. "Her name's Al, but she's a girl."

"My babies are Fiona and Xerxes." She whirled around. "Sit, Fiona! Sit, Xerxes!" They backed down and cocked their heads. Very obedient, but how can you be sure about Dobermans?

"I hope you boys don't have bicycles that you ride on the sidewalks."

"We didn't bring bikes," Luke said. "We're from California."

"Ah, yes." The old lady nodded. "I could see you

weren't very well behaved." Then she whipped around. "Xerxes! You know we do that in the gutter!"

Luke pulled an extra Baggie out of his shorts pocket and handed it to her. Then we got out of there. As we were crossing the street to our house, she yelled out, "You may call on me someday. I'm Miss Hazeltine, and I live right here!"

It made me wonder about New Yorkers. They can turn you in to the police and invite you to a party, almost in the same paragraph.

"That'll be the day," I muttered to Luke.

"Actually, we've seen her before."

"Are you kidding? I'd have remembered."

"We saw her this morning," Luke said. "She was up in the window of that house, getting dressed to go to work. Of course she was about sixty years younger at the time." He was carrying Al. He carried her all the way home.

When we got there, Luke yelled down to Mom and Dad in the kitchen. "We took Al out! She did her business at the corner!"

We went upstairs to wash our hands. When we were coming back down, I almost freaked out on the second floor. This ghostly dead-white figure was right there by the steps before I could think. I came close to a scream.

But it was only Heidi. "Chad? Luke? You haven't been messing around with the stuff in my room, have you?"

"Who, us?" we said.

She ushered us down there, and her room looked regular to me: romance books throughout, the *Top Gun* poster, unmade bed. Luke walked straight to the table next to it. I followed. I was getting almost used to following him.

There was nothing on the table but a gray pile of something, gray and fine as ashes. When I looked closer over Luke's shoulder, I saw. It was the little bouquet of dried crocuses she'd shown us yesterday. But it was more than dry now. It was dried up, turned to dust, and ready to blow away. It looked old and cold.

Where there'd been leaves around the flowers, there were just leaf skeletons now. The ribbon was still there, but you had to look twice. The gold paper letters were gone, like mice had eaten them for the glue. You could barely make out some of the pale outline of the words that had been there.

W   H RESP   TF   AFFE T   N
T.

The sunlight was beaming in. But looking at the dust pile that had been a bouquet of crocuses yesterday was like looking into a coffin or something. It was like something had happened to time.

Heidi was behind us, hanging back. "I'm like I can't believe this. It had to have happened when I was up in the attic, or just now when I was in the bathroom. My bouquet just . . . crumbled away. What's it mean?"

"Heidi, you've got me," I said. "I wish I knew."
But I lied. I didn't want to know.

She stuck close to us on the way down to breakfast. "I'm not meeting Jocelyn till lunch," she said. "She sleeps late. I think she goes out at night to clubs and places. She's got ID. I'm not meeting her till later. What are you guys going to do?"

Us guys? I could tell right there she wasn't about to hang around this house, even in daylight. I know when Heidi's desperate.

She was still with us when we walked Mom over to meet Jocelyn's mom, who was a high-profile real estate agent. Mom wanted to see Mary Lou in action, so we were going to meet her at a fancy Park Avenue address where she was trying to sell an apartment.

After Dad left for work, the rest of us started off down Seventy-third Street. "We haven't been out together like this for years," Mom said, "not since Luke was still in a stroller. I used to take you all along with me to shop at Pick 'n Save because I couldn't get a sitter during the day. This makes me feel young again."

She looked it too. She had on her gold earrings like little X's and her PTA suit. "You're looking good, Mom," I told her.

"I better," she said. "Did you see how well Mary Lou dresses? Very New York. Everything from Bergdorf's."

"You've got her beat a mile," I said. "Remember, you were Rose Queen, not Mary Lou."

"But she was runner-up," Mom said.

When we found the apartment building on Park Avenue, it was like a movie. Doormen in long coats. Stretch limos at the curb. Jocelyn's mom was waiting outside for us. She had on a suit with big shoulders and carried a briefcase, Gucci.

"Dressed for success," Mom murmured.

Mary Lou gave us all a big smile, but if she noticed that Heidi was beginning to look like Jocelyn, she didn't say so. She put her cheek up against Mom's and kissed the air near her ear, which seems to be the New York way.

But she was very professional as she led us into the building. Even the little bows on her shoes were all business. "Apartment two-C," she said to the doorman. "I have the key."

The lobby was full of mirrors and had a lot of class. "This is an all-cash building," Mary Lou explained. "If I can nail a buyer for two-C, I'm looking at a thirty-five-thousand-dollar commission. I've got an exclusive on this one, so I've got to hook a client and reel him in before the sharks start circling."

She could talk without moving her jaw, too, so either Jocelyn inherited that from her, or they both went to the same school.

Apartment 2-C was up a short flight of marble steps just off the lobby. Mary Lou unlocked double doors, and we were right inside the apartment itself. It was as big as a mansion.

"A two-level duplex format," Mary Lou said, practicing on us. "Embassy-scaled drawing room, formal dining room seats thirty-six, solarium—the usual. On the second level, six chambers with connecting baths. All traditional and needs some fluffing up. Furniture available to the buyer."

Luke liked it. If he'd had three million, he'd have bought it himself. It was his kind of place, traditional. All the walls were old polished wood, everything authentic. There was even a suit of armor. Mary Lou led Mom and Heidi into the drawing room, mentioning all the points of interest. I could tell Luke wanted us to explore around on our own.

"Not bad, right?" I said. But he was already over by the wall, poking at a little brass button past the suit of armor. A door flew open. It was a private elevator. He stepped in, and I hurried to catch up. The door closed, and it was the size of a broom closet in there. Luke pushed a button, and we went up to the floor where the six chambers were.

Lights burned in the upstairs hallway, and daylight fell through the open bedroom doors. It was a little creepy, like breaking and entering, but interesting. Pictures of somebody's ancestors hung on the walls. Luke wanted to see everything, so we went on down the hall. There was a closed door at the end. The knob was bigger than his hand and squeaked when he turned it.

Just as the door opened, I smelled burning. Logs on a fire. It was a library. The curtains were closed, and the flames from the fireplace glowed on the dark wood of the walls. A high-back chair was pulled up to the fire. Luke was wandering into the room when I saw the feet. These two feet in carpet slippers were propped up on a footstool between the chair and the fire. I started backpedaling and reached out to snag Luke by the shirt and missed.

An old man looked around the wing of the chair, straight at us. His face was saggy, with a sparse stand of white hair on top. "Who might you two scamps be?" he said in this weird, echoing voice.

"I'm Luke." He pointed a thumb over his head back at me. "That's my brother, Chad."

The old man squinted at us over his glasses. "What's your business here? I'm old. I need peace and quiet. You don't look like any of my grandchildren. Are you?"

Luke shook his head. "We're just having a look around. It's a nice place you've got here."

The old man's jaw dropped, and you could see he didn't have his teeth in. "You better believe it's a nice place. This is an all-cash building, you know. We don't let just anybody in here."

He tried to stare Luke down and failed. "Come on around here closer to the fire," the old man said. "I'll get a crick in my neck." He had on a robe and a scarf. "It's cold for May."

Actually it was late June and close to a heat wave, but Luke let that go.

"Who let you two in here anyway, wandering around like you owned the place?" The old man's eyes were

just watery slits now, and he was really excited. He had
a cane tucked into his chair, and I wanted to keep out of
its range.

"Jocelyn's mom," Luke explained, and I had the idea
he was telling too much. "Her name's Mary Lou. She's a
real-estate agent, and—"

"A *what*?" The old man thrashed around in his chair,
looking for his cane. "How'd a real-estate agent get in
here? Those people are like roaches! Did my son-in-law
send for her? I'm not selling! Nobody sells Pendleton's
place till Pendleton says so, and I'm Pendleton! You cut
out of here and tell them all I'm not selling! A real-
estate agent? Why, I oughta—"

We cut out. I had Luke by the arm, out the door,
down the hall, into the elevator. We dropped a floor, the
door opened, and we stepped out in the front hall directly behind Mom. The elevator door closed behind
us. Heidi noticed our sudden return, but she just rolled
her eyes at the ceiling.

Mary Lou was still giving her real-estate speech.
"The second floor is your standard set of well-propor-
tioned bedrooms and a study with working fireplace.
Terribly good space, though only for the upper-price-
range buyer."

"When can the buyer move in?" Luke piped up.

Mom leapt when she realized we were right there
behind her, and Mary Lou said, "Oh, at once. This is an
estate sale."

"What's that?" Luke asked.

"It means that the former owner, Mr. Pendleton, died."

I thought that was a pretty amazing oversight, since he was still upstairs, thrashing around for his cane. "But," I said, "he's—"

"Passed away toward the end of May, did he?" Luke said.

"That's right," Mary Lou said. "The property is being sold by his executor."

Luke poked me. "She means the son-in-law," he said out of the corner of his mouth.

"Where have you boys been?" Mom said. "You didn't touch anything, did you?"

"Not a thing, Mom." And I was really ready to go. Heidi was already leaving, heading out the door to meet Jocelyn. Mary Lou and Mom were planning lunch and a tour of Mary Lou's office. So this looked as good a time as any for Luke and me to get going.

Mom didn't really want us to wander around town on our own, but Mary Lou came to the rescue. She mentioned that the New York crime rate is a lot lower than your average suburban shopping-mall parking lot. Mom crumbled, and the next thing I remember, Luke and I were out of there, walking down Park Avenue. Even with the car fumes, it was good to be breathing outdoor air.

We stopped for lunch at a counter somewhere, but mainly we kept walking. And I could still feel the atmosphere of Old Man Pendleton's apartment lingering back there behind us.

When we came up on the General Motors Building, I saw they were displaying new cars in the lobby. They wouldn't let you sit inside the cars unless you looked old enough to buy one, but we hung around all of them and picked up a few brochures. I'd probably be there yet, kicking tires, but Luke was beginning to droop. He was tired of the cars, and I'd about walked his legs off. I didn't know what to do with him.

We went outside to sit on some concrete steps. In New York people pretty much sit on steps anywhere. Some of them live there. We watched the crowds go by. All the way down Fifth Avenue guys in crocheted hats were selling Rolex watches for $29.95.

"You still hungry? You want some ice cream or something?"

Luke shook his head. He was sitting on the step with his elbows on his knees and his chin in his fists and one Nike sock down. "I'm sleepy," he said. "I could do with a nap."

A nap? He hadn't taken naps since kindergarten, and he didn't like them then.

"Well, fine," I said. "Why don't you just take a little nap here? Go ahead. I'll wait."

"Are you kidding me?" Luke said, really drooping now. "This is a public place. How could you nap here?"

Right on cue we witnessed a fender-bender at the intersection. Squealing brakes, metal meeting, a front bumper knocked off. Two cabs, and both drivers are out on Fifth, taking swings at each other. Then a passenger from each cab got out, two ladies, and they started swinging at each other with purses. Luke had a point. This was kind of a busy area for a nap.

"Hey, what about F.A.O. Schwarz?" I said. "It's right here in the General Motors Building. It's the greatest toy store in New York. You could . . . look at the toys."

Luke drooped.

"And farther down Fifth is Rockefeller Center. That's a must. If we keep going, there's the Empire State Building. Maybe we'll get lucky and see King Kong up on it, batting down biplanes."

Luke gave me a sideways look. "Chad, sooner or later we have to go home."

True. I turned up my palms. I'm cool. "Fine. But before we go, Luke, let's work out a few things. Remember those soldiers in the park, all dressed up?"

He nodded.

"Well, this is New York, right? They were probably all actors in a play. A movie, maybe. They were probably on location in the park."

"It's possible," Luke said.

"And this morning in the attic. We look out and think we see the Hotel Car—this building being built. But the window wasn't clean, and the lighting was tricky. It could have been an optical illusion."

He was just staring up at me, patient.

"And now we come to that apartment back there.

Look, I can't exactly explain it, but they made some kind of mistake. I mean, it's a big apartment. Maybe they just *thought* Old Man Pendleton was dead. Maybe they didn't—check all the rooms. I've got it. Maybe his son-in-law is so anxious to sell, he's letting Mary Lou scout out the place ahead of time. Maybe the son-in-law's real greedy."

Luke watched my lips. He fidgeted, too, on the hard concrete.

"So okay," I said. "Let's go home."

Al was scratching on the inside of the door before I could get it open. Then when I was reaching around for the burglar alarm, she was all over us, wild to go out. We walked her down to the corner, and then she set all four paws, and we had to drag her home again. She was trying to tell us she wasn't happy in that house, and I knew the feeling.

Back inside it was a shadowy late afternoon. Luke headed upstairs around the big bird cage on the way to his bed. I followed him all the way to his room.

"Go ahead with your nap," I said. "I'll just hang out in here and—keep you company."

"Whatever," he said, half asleep. I got down on the floor to play with Al, but she was too jumpy. She shot under the bed, and when I tried to pull her out, she took a swipe at me. I know I went to sleep because I woke up with a bang.

Luke's feet, still in Keds, hit the floor by my ear. He

was up, looking around, bright eyed. "What was that?" he said. "Did you hear anything?"

"Like what?"

"I don't know. Voices. The house." He was wide awake now. "I did enough sleeping anyway."

"Have you been dreaming?"

"I don't know," he said. "It doesn't matter. Come on." He was stepping over me. "We've got to stop wasting time. There's so much to do, and take care of. There are these people in the house."

I was really beginning to hate it when he said things like that. And I thought he might need a half an aspirin. He was all riled up.

"Come on, Chad. Let's go back upstairs again." He worked his hands together like he couldn't wait to get them on that padlock.

"Not the attic again, Luke. We've seen all there is to see up there. Forget it."

He just lifted his shoulders. "Okay. I just thought it might be safer."

Safer? What did he mean by safer?

"I mean, what if we went upstairs again, and we got all the way back to . . . then? To the time when people lived here before. I thought maybe the girls in the aprons wouldn't be up there. Maybe they'd all be downstairs working and not in their rooms. How do I know if they can see us? Sure, Old Mr. Pendleton saw us, but he just died a few weeks ago. He may not even know he's dead." Luke gazed up at me and blinked twice.

Somehow I felt better. This was beginning to sound more and more like an average kid with a big imagination. I smiled at him. I ought to lighten up.

When he started down the hall, I caught up with him. He slowed down and stopped at the top of the stairwell, sensing the house. I still wanted this to be a game. We started down the stairs and stopped again on the hall one floor down. One way was Mom and Dad's room, with the door open. The other way was Heidi's, with the door shut. Luke went that way. The thought of that dried-up bouquet crossed my mind.

When his hand was on the knob of her door, I said, "Maybe Heidi came home early."

He shook his head. "Nobody's in there, not now." He turned the knob, and the door swung back, slow.

Before I saw, I felt the blast of cold. It wasn't the central air-conditioning turned up, and it wasn't wind. It was the deadly cold of a closed space, like a meat locker or something. I wanted to grab Luke and pull him back, but my hands felt frozen. I looked into Heidi's room, and I'd never been in there in my life.

It was another room from another time. Another season, even. The carpet was gone, and the vertical blinds were off the windows. There were different curtains, and an incredible winter scene outside. The panes were frosted over, but you could see the gray shapes of the snow built up on the sills. It was one mean winter day with more snow than Tahoe.

All of Heidi's things were gone, but the room was furnished—crammed. A brass bed against out-of-date wallpaper with greenish ivy leaves. A big old dresser, an old rowing machine, everything in heavy, dark wood.

I was holding Luke back, and he was letting me. We saw enough from the doorway. A pair of ice skates with curly runners on the rag rug by the bed. Underneath it was a big china pot. Old pennants and class pictures hung on the ivy walls. Books, too, in glass-fronted bookcases. Not Heidi's romance books. These were real ones, leather-looking.

There was a lot more, all shadowy but absolutely real. It was a guy's room with all his stuff, a hockey stick, high-topped leather shoes. Neckties and separate collars hung on his dresser mirror along with a stiff straw hat, waiting for some summer. On the wicker table was the only thing I recognized: a bouquet of yellow flowers. Little crocuses nipped and preserved in this Arctic air.

The cold was forming on my face, and I couldn't take it anymore. I had Luke in a hammerlock. I reached past him and pulled the door shut. This side of it had a new knob and fresh paint. The hallway was climate controlled. We were back in our century.

"We didn't see that," I said.

He didn't bother to answer.

"We're still too late," he said.

"Late?" I said in a breaking voice. "What do you mean *late*? That was a hundred years ago in there. How far back do we have to go, dinosaurs?"

The front doorbell rang. I leapt. But Luke looked around me down the normal hall, interested. It was a jangle of real bells. But I thought: *Fine, I can handle this. It's Mom and Heidi, and for some reason they've forgotten their house keys.* Luke was by the stairwell now, looking over the railing down to the front hall. I started his way, but he put up a finger to keep me quiet.

Beside him I could see part of the hall downstairs. But it wasn't our hall anymore. It was like Heidi's room. We seemed to have striped wallpaper down there now and old varnished floors. Somebody was there. This figure was walking along the hall from the back of the house.

It was a girl in an apron and a frilly cap. She walked right past the big bird cage. Her skirts were long. They broke over the round toes of her shoes as she walked on a red carpet I'd never seen before. It was a maid going to answer the door, and she was real, as real as we were. Maybe more so.

Seven

She was past us now, and I could hear my heart. Luke tugged at my hand, and we crept down a short flight, around the landing behind the bird cage. We were on the last flight down to the hall and could see through the brass bars all the way to the front of the house.

The maid pulled open the door. Two people stood out on the stoop, silhouettes against the afternoon. A woman and a girl. The woman's skirts went down to the doorsill. The girl's skirts almost did. Their hats overlapped. The maid bobbed a curtsy and stepped aside.

"Really, Pegeen, you are slow as molasses," the lady said.

"Yes, Mrs. Dunlap." The maid worked around to help them off with their cloaks.

It was a brisk day with a breeze coming down the hall. It wasn't like Heidi's room upstairs, frozen hard with winter. This was another season, with the smell of fall leaves in bonfires somewhere.

The girl and her mother were unbuttoning their gloves, lifting the veils off their faces. They turned to a blank wall, which must have a mirror on it now. They were looking into it as they pulled the pins out of their hats.

I nearly knew the girl. I'd seen her before. She'd

been out on the stoop in the early morning yesterday when the milkman came. Now I saw she was beautiful, even in this outfit and the boots that buttoned up her legs under the skirt. Her hair was pale and smooth and fell over the big sleeves of her shiny brown dress. She was maybe the most beautiful girl I'd ever seen.

"Tea in the front parlor, I think, Pegeen," her mother said.

And I froze. Pegeen turned back toward us. We were up only a couple of steps. We were almost in the open, and I didn't want to try any fast move.

But she turned down the stairs on the other side of the bird cage, heading to the basement kitchen. I had the idea there were other girls in aprons working down there. I heard things—spoons stirring.

The woman and the girl had gone into the front parlor. At this point I started doing things to myself, like biting the inside of my cheek to prove I was awake, even alive. I looked down at myself. I had on my big thrasher shirt from Rip City. I was wearing my Banana Republic pants with the extra pockets, my L.A. Gear running shoes. It was the regular me, and Luke too.

He was creeping down the last steps and walking carefully along this old red rug toward the parlor door. To be on the safe side he wasn't making a sound. They don't call them sneakers for nothing.

I caught up with him, but we didn't go in the front room. We didn't have to. Against the wall in the hall stood this fancy old combination hat rack, umbrella stand, and mirror. We could see some of the front parlor in its reflection.

My eyes bugged out of my head. It was a jungle in there: big red furniture, green ferns in pots, a bamboo tree. A fancy brass chandelier had fat light bulbs that came to points. The only familiar thing reflected in the mirror was the marble fireplace. There were a lot of family pictures on the mantel. Not our family.

The mother, Mrs. Dunlap, had sat down, but I could see the girl pacing back and forth in front of the hearth.

"Really, Mama, it is too provoking," she said. "We have gone to all the trouble to hire a trap and a pair *and* a footman, if you please. And all we have done this livelong afternoon is to drive up to Fifth Avenue and Seventy-ninth Street to leave a card on those Ebersoles. We have better things to do with our time and worthier persons to call on."

The mother murmured.

I recognized the girl's voice. It was almost as familiar to me as she was, but I couldn't place it. Out in the hall Luke and I weren't breathing.

"Truly, Mama," she said, "I am at my wit's end about that brother of mine. It is enough that Tyler goes around with calf's eyes, thinking he is in love with Consuelo Ebersole. *Now* he expects you and me, the women of his family, to leave a calling card at that vulgar great mansion of theirs."

"Still, I would like to have seen inside the Ebersole mansion, Emily," the mother said.

Emily. The girl's name was Emily.

"Mama, you have had a narrow escape. Mrs. Ebersole would likely look down her nose at you if you ever met. They are much too rich. And by comparison we are the dust beneath their feet. As for Consuelo, it's well known that she is a terrible snob. The trouble with Tyler is that he does not know the difference between Fifth Avenue and Seventy-third Street."

"Your father is going to speak to Tyler, Emily. I am sure he will set the boy on the right path."

Emily stamped her boot on the tiles. "Men!" she said. "When men get together, Mama, it is the blind leading the blind."

"Well, my dear," Mrs. Dunlap said, "where would *you* lead your brother?"

Emily was ready for this. "Not far at all, Mama. Only across the street to number twenty-nine. I would lead Tyler straight up to Mamie Vanderdonk's door. Mamie is the kind of girl any young man would be privileged to pay his court to."

"She is very young, of course," Mrs. Dunlap said.

"Mama, she is all but sixteen, just two years ahead of me at the Brearley. And so she is but two years younger than Tyler. That is nothing in the years ahead, and she is exactly the sister-in-law I would like to have. We are already best friends. I picture quite a long engagement while Tyler gets his education at Yale. And then a wedding with myself as maid of honor. These very parlors would be ideal for the wedding reception. I see them banked in orange blossoms, with Pegeen and the others doing the serving."

"How thorough you are, Emily," her mother remarked.

"Mama, if I do not plan, Tyler will have his heart broken by that Consuelo Ebersole. You know yourself the Ebersoles would never allow Tyler to have her. They'll hope to marry her off to some dreary European title. And if that doesn't work, they wouldn't let her go to anybody less than an Astor or a Vanderbilt, families of that sort. They would certainly look no lower than a Roosevelt."

"It is true that Mamie is a fine girl," Mrs. Dunlap said. "And the Vanderdonks are much more our sort of people. But, Emily, life is rarely that simple."

"I will tell you who's simple, Mama. It's my brother Tyler who's simple. Simple-minded."

Meanwhile out in the hall I got the biggest shock of my life to date. I heard something behind me, whirled around, and Pegeen was bearing down on us. She was balancing a big silver tray with a lot of things on it. She was almost within reach and moving. I could hear her breathing, and I had zero time to think.

When I kneed Luke in the back, he shot forward across the parlor door. I leapt and fell over him. Then I tried to scoot us both out of the way to keep Pegeen from stepping on us. Or, who knows—through us. I still didn't know if she could see us. The tray could have been in the way.

Luke was flat out on the floor, and our arms and legs were all tangled up. It was like the Lakers.

"Tea, Mrs. Dunlap."

"Pegeen, you are slow as—"

I thought I might have broken Luke's face when I jammed him down on that walnut floor. But he was recovering. His head was coming up out of oyster-white carpeting. Somebody was standing over us, throwing a shadow. Somewhere past her I noticed the front door was open. It was Heidi with a couple of shopping bags.

"Why are you two fighting?"

Luke and I were both up now, shaky on our pins. He was tucking his shirt into his shorts. I was feeling fuzzy. "I was just showing him a couple wrestling holds," I said.

She gave me a look and did something with her black lips. "Where's Mom?"

"Whose?" I said.

"Ours, of course."

"Oh. Well, she's not home yet," I said. "It's just . . . us. What's that in your ears?"

She had new earrings, which seemed to be nuts, bolts, and nails soldered together. She had on a whole new outfit: prison gray with darker stripes. An empty cartridge belt held up her baggy shorts.

"Jocelyn and I shopped," she said. "Nothing I've got works here." She wandered on upstairs.

We watched her go, but all I could think of was how

glad I was to be back in the twentieth century. Luke led me into the front parlor, and it looked fine: completely carpeted, neutral walls, glass tabletops, nothing over the mantel but the picture of dots. No strange old chandelier, just track lighting. But Luke was gazing up at me, testing me. He wondered if I was going to tell him we hadn't seen anything.

"Yeah, well it was . . . interesting," I said. "Like a . . . play."

He kept gazing at me. "It wasn't a play, Chad. It was happening."

I hated to admit it, but he had a point. We'd smelled the autumn leaves burning outside. We'd hit the polished floor hard. I'd seen Emily, heard her.

"In one way it was like a play," Luke said quietly. "We have to see it through. We have to know how it ends."

"I don't see why," I said. "Emily wants her brother to fall for Mamie. He's crazy about that other girl, Consuelo. What business is it of ours? It was all a long time ago."

"That's not the problem," Luke said. "You know that if you think about it."

After dinner that night Dad said we ought to go on another family walk. Heidi wasn't going. I guess she was willing to tough it out in the house on the chance Thor Desmond might call. The rest of us went, taking Al.

Mom and Dad strolled along, arm in arm, as Luke led

us up Fifth Avenue. Central Park was off on our left across the stream of Yellow Cabs. The apartment buildings along here were all top of the line, like Old Man Pendleton's over on Park Avenue. Al would have trotted all the way to Harlem, but Luke reined her in at the Seventy-ninth Street corner. He was watching me again. Across the intersection a tremendous high-rise stood forty stories tall. A drive curved up in front with cabs pulling in and doormen opening doors. Luke kept looking back and forth between me and it.

We turned around to start back down Fifth, and there to the south of us was the Empire State Building. Its tower was lighted red, white, and blue because the Fourth of July was coming up. Mom and Dad were ahead of us now, and Luke poked me. He pointed a little thumb over his shoulder. I looked back.

There was no forty-story high-rise on the Seventy-ninth Street corner. No cabs, no stoplights, nothing like that. It was some completely different night because an old house like a wedding cake stood there, a castle with copper roofs. It blazed with yellow light through long, looping curtains. The driveway was there, curving up, with carriages. Horses stamped, and the carriages were neat boxes on wheels. Men in high hats and women who glittered were climbing the steps to a front door. The shrubbery up by the house was lightly dusted with snow.

I looked away quick, and there down Fifth, the

Empire State Building stood a hundred and two stories high in the summer night.

"How do we *do* that, Luke?"

"I don't know." He turned up his hands. "I'm only eight."

I glanced across Fifth Avenue at the park, which looked dark and dangerous. "It's getting on my nerves."

"The Ebersoles lived in that big mansion," Luke said. "Consuelo and her parents. Emily's probably right. I bet they're snooty."

We were ambling south behind Mom and Dad, and I was looking straight ahead. "Don't talk about those people as if they're alive."

"But they are," he said. "They're alive in their time."

"Well, their time isn't our time, and you can't go back and forth. It's not normal, and it's . . . weird."

"Scary, you mean," he said. "It'll be worse than that if we can't help them. It'll be this big disaster of some kind if we can't help them."

"Who?"

"You know who. Tyler. Emily."

So I wouldn't walk with him anymore. I moved up with Dad, and he went over on Mom's other side.

Back home Dad said we ought to catch a movie in the home entertainment room off the back parlor. In our video disc library he'd discovered all three *Star Wars* movies, special edition in uncropped image and full digital sound. So we were all set.

I could really get into this, sitting near Mom and Dad in a room full of twentieth-century high tech. Luke lasted about twenty minutes. He slipped out of the room, and I thought about letting him go. But then I followed

When I started up the stairs, I found him on the first landing behind the phone booth. He had his elbows on the banister, and he was staring at the brass bars of the cage with a faraway look in his eyes.

"You know what this thing is?" He reached over the railing and tapped a brass bar on the cage. "It was here in the house in the old days. The Dunlaps must have put it in."

"They put it in when they got their first telephone?"

He shook his head. "It wasn't a phone booth then. It was an elevator. One of the first. The Dunlaps were pretty up-to-date people. They had electricity and everything."

"If this was an elevator," I said, "where are the cables for it?"

Luke looked up the dark stairwell above us. "They used to be up there. They were there this afternoon when we—"

"Well, that's pretty interesting."

"Important too," he said, "but I'm not sure why. Lots of things about the past are like memories that just slipped my mind. I need practice. We both do."

"Wait a minute—"

"Take this morning, for example. When we ran into

Old Mr. Pendleton, that was pure carelessness. Slipping back just a few weeks in time isn't going to get us anyplace. Probably anybody could do that. And remember the attic? There we were in 1929, and so what? We didn't have any business there."

I looked around like the walls could be listening. Maybe they could.

"Luke, we don't have business back in any of those old times."

"Sure we do," he said. "If we didn't, we wouldn't have the gift."

Some gift. "Maybe it's just dietary, Luke. Maybe we've got a chemical imbalance or something. In my case it could just be puberty."

Luke shook his head. "I don't think puberty's this interesting. Do you want to see where Emily's room was?"

He climbed on up to the second floor. At the end of the hall was a line of light under Heidi's door. But Luke stopped at the top of the stairs. He pointed at the blank wall in front of us. "I think Emily's room was right through there."

"You mean there was a door here once? What's on the other side? Isn't it Mom and Dad's bathroom and Heidi's bathroom and a couple of dressing rooms?"

He nodded. "People didn't have so much plumbing in those days. Mr. and Mrs. Dunlap had the front room, like Mom and Dad. Tyler was at the back where Heidi is. Emily must have been here in between. We have the

Dunlaps' guest rooms upstairs, Chad. That's why the voices we hear at night sound farther off. At least it's a possibility."

"This house is full of possibilities," I said. "Too many."

"Want to try to see if we can find Emily's room?" Luke slipped his hand into mine. "We saw Tyler's this afternoon without even trying, hardly."

"No, Luke. I don't."

"We've got to keep trying," he said. "We've got to get things . . . fine tuned. When we saw Tyler's room, it was already too late, and he was . . . gone."

Gone?

"Then this afternoon when Emily and her mom were having tea, that was a little early."

Early?

"Then tonight when we saw the Ebersoles' mansion, and they were having a party—"

"Okay, Luke. Okay. You're overloading my circuits."

We were heading toward Mom and Dad's bedroom door. "Besides," he said, "maybe you'll get to see Emily again, which is something you'd like to do."

We didn't turn on the light in the front bedroom. We just wheeled around into Mom and Dad's bathroom and flipped on the lights in there. It was a good bathroom with Jacuzzi tub and double sinks, black marble and chrome throughout, and more folded towels than you'd need.

Luke stood in the middle of the new marble floor, gazing around. We didn't seem to be anywhere near

Emily's room and century, but then you never know. There were louvered double doors at the back of the bathroom. Luke tried to squint through the slats. Then he reached for the two small knobs and pushed both doors open into darkness. I couldn't see anything, but I was ready to grab him back.

"Maybe we better not—"

But he found a light switch, and this new room lit up. A thin guy in spit-shined wingtip shoes, a summer suit, and no head appeared to be standing in the corner. It was what Dad was going to wear to work in the morning, hanging on his clothes rack. Mirrored doors led into Mom's area. It was his-and-hers dressing rooms, very modern. You could smell the mothproofing.

"Let's call it a night, Luke."

But I heard the same sound he did, a humming like far-off locusts. It came from behind one more door at the rear of the dressing room. The door was closed, but Luke gave it a shove.

White light blinded me. I made a leap for him, and we were in another room before we could get stopped. White tile in here and glowing bulbs around all the mirrors. A load of clutter on the counter top. The humming in our ears was louder, a roar. Half blind, I saw the flash of a steel blade, two of them.

"Don't!" I yelled.

And she didn't. Heidi. It was her bathroom Luke and I had just rocketed into. The scissors fell from her hand and clattered on the counter top. The roar was from her hair dryer, still plugged in. She was just about to give herself a haircut like Jocelyn's—a Beastie Boy short on the sides and nothing much left on top. The sudden sight of us left her speechless. So was Luke. All he could do was stare.

Heidi had already dyed her flowing California-blond hair Jocelyn-black. It really changed her, and it was still half wet. I wondered if it would dry blacker.

"Aren't you supposed to cut your hair first and then dye it?" I said, glad she hadn't.

"I don't know." She didn't have a stitch on except a towel. Little rivers of black dye ran down from her head and over her collarbones. "I was in a hurry or something."

I knew I'd never adjust to her with coal-black hair. And believe me, neither would Dad.

"Hey, Heidi, don't you know that girls with Jocelyn's hair color want to be blondes?"

"Not this year they don't," she said. "Jocelyn's on the cutting edge of fashion." She gave us a little nod, which meant Luke and I were supposed to get out of her bathroom.

"Just don't cut anything off, okay?"

". . . Okay," she said, but her eyes were on her reflection in the mirror, with her hair like this big dark cloud around her head. And her mind was somewhere else, way off where I couldn't begin to read it.

We filed out through her bedroom on the way to the hall. It was definitely her room, not Tyler's. The music coming off her tape deck was Sting's "Bring on the Night." One of her paperbacks was cracked open on her bed: *Hilary and Hank, a Halftime Romance.* It all looked okay to me—not very tidy, but definitely Heidi.

Out in the hall Luke stumbled along, yawning.

"Listen," I said, "we ought to try not to dream. Or if we happen to hear, like, voices, we ought to just ignore them. Let's let . . . bygones be bygones. What if we got into their world, really got into it? Let's not open any more doors. What if we couldn't get back?"

"It's a possibility," he said, starting up the stairs to the third floor. And that was the night that Emily came to me.

Eight

The whole house seemed like one big ear, alive and listening. I took my time getting into bed and then I tried to stay awake. But that never works, and I kept hearing the house. The regular sounds of an old place: creaking beams, popping floorboards, something like sighing.

Then I was sound asleep and, I guess, dreaming. But it was at least as real as being awake. It had to be a dream, though. I was six feet tall and shaved. I was even wearing a double-breasted blue blazer of Dad's, and it fit in the shoulders. Definitely a dream.

I knew right where I was. The Ebersole mansion, their private ballroom. I'd never seen it before, but I knew every corner of it, a gold-and-ivory room. I dream in color.

It was a big party with a full orchestra playing the waltzes of old Vienna. The bandleader was Sting. Since it was a masquerade party, everybody wore fancy evening clothes and masks. I was the only one in the room without a mask. In most dreams you're dressed all wrong, if you're dressed at all.

You're usually looking for someone, and I was. But everywhere I turned, there were masks like birds, with feathers and glittering eyes. I saw a girl in the wildest mask of all, crusty with diamonds. Her long neck was roped with pearls. So it had to be Consuelo.

But I wasn't looking for her. The dancers parted, and Emily was there in the center of the room. She wasn't dressed for the occasion either. She was masked like the others, but I recognized the smooth pale hair that fell over the shoulders of her shiny brown dress. Her skirts didn't sweep the misty floor, and her boots buttoned up.

Then I was holding her in my arms like I'd never held a girl. That was the realest part. We were dancing, and I don't know how. But Sting's arrangement of "The Beautiful Blue Danube" caught us in its undertow, and we floated just above the floor. By now I was fighting to stay asleep. Emily watched me through her mask. We turned and turned in the room and never ran into anybody.

So, yes, it was a dream, but by now, who cares? The music was louder, faster, and Emily's mood changed.

"Really, Tyler, I am at the end of my patience with you," she said. I felt her hand squeeze my shoulder.

I looked down, and I was wearing this incredible rig: a long black coat, longer behind. Starchy shirt with a white waistcoat cut low. I couldn't see my tie because it was tucked up under my chin, but a gold watch chain hung in loops across my middle. My shoes were black and shiny and came to points.

"Tyler, are you listening?" Emily said. To me.

I nodded. Or I'd become Tyler, and he nodded. Something like that.

"Mark well my words, Brother," Emily said, "for you must make your choice for all times, and it had better be the right one."

The music was turned way up, pounding my head.

"Choose carefully, Tyler, for it is a matter of life or—"

She broke from me, and I thought she was gone for good. I'd have turned away, except in dreams you don't have options. Then she was back with two other girls. One of them was Consuelo, tall and proud with milky shoulders and glittering diamonds.

But there was somebody else, small, in a snow-white dress that might do for a wedding. Not a diamond on her, just a few rosebuds on her skirts. A wholesome type of girl. Emily waved her forward almost into my arms. "Will it be Mamie?"

But I didn't have time to choose. My timing was off.

"Or . . . Consuelo?"

Consuelo didn't need any encouragement. She came at me like she owned the world, and maybe she did. Her hand dripping with diamonds came out for mine. The rest of the room faded, and Consuelo was lowering her mask. I opened my mouth to scream. My hands came up, Tyler's did, trying to cover my eyes.

Behind Consuelo's mask was a skull scoured of all flesh. No, it was worse than that. It was a skull turned brown by time and stained by the graveyard years. I looked around me, and everybody in the fading ballroom was like her. All their masks were lowered now, and skulls stared at me because all of these people were dead, long dead. And I had no business being here. The sockets of their empty eyes were deep black tunnels where I heard screams echoing into eternity. When I dream, I *dream.*

A hand closed over my pointed, shiny-leather foot. I was going to be dragged down into someplace deep. And I was yelling my head off.

I sat up in bed, hoarse already. Dad was there at the end of the bed. He'd been shaking my foot, but he'd jumped back.

"Do you wake up like that every morning?" he said. He was wearing a sweatband and an Izod shirt and shorts. "Let's have a run in the park, Chad. You look like you need to get the kinks out."

I had to get my running stuff on, do all my bathroom things. But still I beat him down to the front door. It was early. We had time for an hour's run before Dad even had to think about getting to work. It was great, another of those perfect mornings, everything one hundred percent real.

We did some bends and stretches at the Fifth Avenue corner and crossed at the light on Seventy-second. We were in the park with the early runners and a few of the tai-chi people, everybody authentic and three dimensional. We ran over a lot of the park on the running lanes, and I began to sweat out most of the cobwebs in my brain and any dreams I might have been dreaming.

Dad set a loping pace, good for his knees. I kept just ahead, reserving a small edge for myself. By the time we'd made a long loop and were coming back on the Central Park West side, his Izod was soaked through.

By the Strawberry Fields he was sucking wind like a drowning man. But when we took a break, and I flopped down, he pretended to jog in place for about two seconds. Then he crashed down too. I wondered if he'd seen Heidi's new hair yet. But why rush things? He checked his watch because it was time to be getting back.

We cut across the park on the Seventy-second Street Transverse and let other runners leave us in the dust, even elderly runners. By the time we were going past the Bethesda Fountain in slow motion, Dad was tripping over small stones, and I could have used a sweatband myself. The day was heating up, and we were weaving to keep in the shade. I was about half blind with salty sweat.

On that last stretch we were coming along past the statue of the Puritan that stands up on a little knoll. I repeat, I was half blind, but I caught sight of a couple of people. They were climbing up this little hill beside the statue. They'd left the pavement and were carrying a big wicker thing like a picnic hamper between them. Two girls.

You couldn't miss them. Everybody else in the park was in running gear or stone-washed cutoffs. These two were a ways off, and yet I could see they were bundled up. And they wore bonnets, big flared ones so you couldn't have seen their faces unless they'd turned completely around. They had on things like capes and long skirts. You couldn't see above their ankles, only the buttons on their boots. They were a strange sight, believe it.

The sun was full on them, and down here at the bottom of the hill bikers were pumping along the Transverse in their black Lycra. And these two girls were climbing the hill in their button boots. I even saw how their gloved hands gripped the handle of the heavy hamper between them. We were moving past them now, but I saw them crest the hill and disappear down the far side. One of them was Emily.

All my cobwebs came back. I was only watching the ground now. Every Popsicle wrapper and crack in the blacktop. I'd have run out onto Fifth Avenue against the light, under a bus, if Dad hadn't pulled me back.

Home in my bathroom I turned up the shower as cold as I could handle it and stayed under as long as possible. I met Dad on the stairs, heading down to breakfast. I was right behind him when he walked into the dining area.

For Luke it was business as usual. He was spooning up Special K and wearing yesterday's T-shirt because I hadn't been there to tell him to change. Mom was by the counter, looking stressed out, trying not to see Heidi.

She sat across from Luke, looking very strange. She's

always had a lot of hair, and now that it was jet black, she looked like that lady on TV who introduces the horror films. Daytime made her hair blacker. She had on the white makeup again and the black lips and the hardware in her ears, and a black sweatshirt, pushed up to show she was wearing biker's bracelets.

It stopped Dad cold. "What in the—"

But Mom shook her head at him.

I edged around in front of them both because sometimes they communicate just by moving their lips, no sound.

Will it shampoo out? Dad mouthed at Mom.

I don't think she's thought that far ahead, Mom's mouth replied.

What am I supposed to do? Act like I don't notice? What? Mom asked.

Never mind. Dad drank a quick cup of coffee at the counter. Heidi sat there, picking seeds out of her orange juice. She knew she'd gone too far, and her black lips were pursed up. There were black smudges on the juice glass, and she seemed pretty sulky. It was like starting the day with Sean Penn.

When I got Luke out of there, he still had a little mustache of orange juice on his upper lip. Usually I get him to brush his teeth after every meal, but we didn't have time.

"Where are we going?" he said.

"To the park. On business."

"Do we take Al?"

"No Al."

That was just as well because when we hit the street, we walked straight into a professional dog-walker. These people take out fifteen or twenty dogs at a time, all on separate leashes. Luke was surrounded by dogs of all sizes. Somehow we both got through, but it would have freaked Al bad. She wasn't over Fiona and Xerxes yet.

"Where in the park?" Luke asked.

"There's this statue of one of the Puritan fathers, which is—"

"I know where it is." He was studying me. "What did you see?"

"Probably nothing."

He was still trying to read me. I told him to keep his eye on the traffic instead. We were crossing Fifth, and some of these cabdrivers don't know red from green. Then we were by the hill. Luke saw me look up at the top. He saw me thinking about forgetting the whole thing.

"Was it Emily?"

I nodded. "And another girl."

"It must have been sudden," he said. "Like a surprise."

"You could say that."

"What were they doing?"

"Maybe going for a picnic. They had on a lot of heavy clothes, gloves even."

"Then it wouldn't have been summer, would it? So it wouldn't have been a picnic."

"I don't know, Luke. I just don't know."

He started up the hill above the park benches full of sunners. The sun turned his hair into corn silk. He'd go without me and was proving it. I caught up with him, but I was still dragged from that morning run. The sun felt like hot wax on the back of my neck.

It wasn't much of a hill. You could see the high-rises of Fifth Avenue behind it and a lot of hot blue sky. A breeze helped, and we were at the top before I realized.

Then I realized. The wind whipped around, coming at us from a new direction. The cold went right to the bone. I looked up, and all the Fifth Avenue high-rises were gone. Nothing but gray, sunless sky. The trees were smaller, and there wasn't a leaf on them, just black branches. I saw that here on the other side of the hill it was winter. The whole world was in winter. Over on Fifth Avenue through the naked trees teams of horses were pulling black carriages. The harnesses jingled with a sharp, winterish sound. They moved along past a row of low mansions. There was snow on the ground, a light dusting. Through my sneaker soles I felt the park frozen hard, crusty.

Luke stopped just out of my reach, staring at the bottom of the hill. He was looking at a long trench dug out among the black trees, like a war. You could see piles of frozen dirt they'd dug out. In a couple of places the trench was roofed with packing-case wood, pitched like roofs. At one point a little tin chimney stood up, spewing smoke.

Over in the trees past the trench little kids were walking around in the white park, muffled up with scarves over their heads. They were picking up sticks and had rags tied around their feet. When I stepped up and put my hands on Luke's shoulders, he was shaking with the cold. But he concentrated on these kids looking for firewood.

"People living in the park?" I said. "Like this?"

He nodded. "They're looking for anything they can use for fuel. They live in that trench."

"This is terrible. This doesn't have anything to do with Emily. When I saw her a while ago, it was probably —some other time."

"Watch." He pointed down where the trench was roofed over.

A head with a bonnet appeared down there just at ground level. A blanket hung over an opening to the roofed part of the trench. She'd twitched it aside and was coming out. She set the big hamper up in the snow, out of the trench. Now she was scrambling out herself. The bonnet turned our way, and I saw Emily's face. She shook out her skirts and reached back to help another girl scramble out.

"Mamie," Luke whispered. "It wouldn't be Consuelo."

Emily hung the empty hamper on her arm. They

were heading back up our way, talking together. Their bonnets funneled together. The last thing I noticed was the sprig of holly with red berries pinned on Emily's cape.

"Come on," I said, grabbing Luke's arm. "Let's cut out. Let's get back to the house while this is still happening. Let's keep it going." Then we were running, flat out, into the past.

Nine

Afterward I never actually remembered how we got home. Was it summer or winter? Now or then? Basically, it was a blur, or both. Our sneakers slapped frozen ground, and I remember matted park grass. People were around, dimmer than a dream, some in Lycra and bikers' gloves, a lady with a fur muff. I don't know.

We didn't look for traffic before crossing Fifth. I think I heard horses' hooves, but I smelled bus exhaust. Then we were pounding down Seventy-third Street, the home stretch: twenty dogs with a professional dog-walker—and a small kid in leggings pulling an old wooden sled. There may have been a steady line of parked cars, but you could smell horse manure. Mainly, it was cold weather and colder as we neared the house. Then we were up the stoop and through the front door like a couple of heat-seeking missiles.

I reached for the switch on the burglar alarm, and my hand splayed against striped wallpaper. The big combination hat rack, umbrella stand, and mirror was there. The long red carpet stretched through the house. When I could catch my breath, I smelled turkey roasting from somewhere below. It was absolutely quiet, and about a hundred years ago.

Luke got in front of me. He was looking around,

listening hard. We saw a corner of the front parlor: a big old whatnot shelf loaded with items. But nobody seemed to be here. It felt like an afternoon, very winterish.

"What if Pegeen heard us come in?"

"It's okay," Luke said. "She's slow as molasses." He started down the hall. Warm light was coming out of the door to the back parlor.

But he stopped. I heard it too. A creaking, wheezy sound about us. Metal clanked. Every hair on my head stood up. We were almost to the stairwell, and I saw the elevator wasn't there, but it was coming. It was creaking down through the house on its cables, rattling a little, and somebody was in it. Through the bars I saw long skirts. We were in the open, too late to go forward or fall back.

The elevator and I shuddered. It came to rest on the main floor. Hands pushed open the little doors from inside, and Emily's mother stepped out. It was Mrs. Dunlap in front of us, and real, absolutely real. We weren't just looking. We were there.

She wore a fine dark red dress with a high collar. She wasn't as pretty as Emily, but she was impressive. Little red stones hung down from her ears. As she stepped out of the elevator, she swept up her skirts with a graceful hand. There was quite a bit behind her, a bustle. She started in the direction of the back parlor, but suddenly turned our way.

We were a couple of statues there, and she looked

right at us, and through us. Frowning a little, she worked her hands together. When we'd come through the door, we'd let in a gust of winter wind. She felt it, but she didn't see us. Her gaze went straight through me and out the back of my head. I felt it slightly.

While we were trying to figure our next move, Mrs. Dunlap made her way down to the back parlor, her bustle moving from side to side. It almost had a life of its own. Luke watched her go, standing there in yesterday's T-shirt and nylon shorts with racing stripes. Then he waved us on.

It was warm in the back parlor. A fire crackled in the hearth. Mrs. Dunlap had settled in a big chair by a rear window. Outside you could see all the way south to Seventy-second Street. There was an open back yard behind the house and a wooden barn. It was about a half-billion dollars' worth of prime East Side Manhattan real estate, except now it was still out in the suburbs with plenty of space.

I'd thought it might be a Sunday afternoon, and now I saw why. It was Christmas. A rope of evergreen hung from the mantel. A tremendous tree glistening with tinsel stood in the corner with its star against the ceiling. Actual wax candles were clipped on the branches, waiting to be lighted.

We'd edged into the room, surer now that Mrs. Dunlap couldn't see us. But we kept our backs to a wall. In front of me Luke pointed to the tall mirror over the fireplace. Two rows of shiny paper letters hung there:

HAPPY CHRISTMAS TO ALL
& A PROSPEROUS 1888

Yes, it was Christmas. Of 1887.

Mrs. Dunlap took some stitches in a piece of needlepoint, angling it to the light from the window. Then the front door of the house banged open. I don't think they locked it in those days.

Emily burst into the room, lighting it up. Her bonnet and cape were off. It was Emily, and we'd just seen her in the park. Her dress was shiny plaid, and though her skirts were above the floor, she had a bustle, a small one.

"Well, Mama, there you sit on Christmas Day, all by your lonesome." She went over to settle on the chair arm, and Mrs. Dunlap turned up her face for a kiss.

It was funny what Emily could do for a room. I'd thought the old times were all black and white like the pictures. But this room was bright. The red in her mother's dress and in Emily's cheeks. Smells too: the Christmas smell of the tree mingling with roasting turkey. It was alive, and more alive with Emily here.

"And Papa's not home yet?"

"Christmas is a workday like any other for a newspaperman," her mother said, "as well you know, Emily."

Emily slumped and swung a foot. "Sometimes I think Papa is married to that *Sun* newspaper instead of to you, Mama."

"Hush," Mrs. Dunlap said, nodding to the door.

Another girl was standing there, not quite certain. It

was the girl with Emily we'd seen carrying the hamper to the trench in the park. She'd taken off her bonnet and was touching her hair.

"Oh, Mamie," Emily said, "come in, for pity's sake."

It was Mamie—Vanderdonk, the girl who lived across the street at number twenty-nine. It was also the girl I'd dreamed about, the one who wasn't Consuelo. But that had only been a dream, so this real Mamie wasn't the same. No mask, of course, and no rosebuds on her dress. She was taller than Emily and older. But she wasn't as sure of herself. Not bad looking, either, but not like Emily. You probably wouldn't notice her so much at first.

"Merry Christmas, Mrs. Dunlap." Her voice was low, like music.

"And a very Merry Christmas to you, too, Mamie. You girls must sit before the fire. You're both chilled through after your errand of charity."

"Mama, please." Emily put up a finger. "It wasn't charity. It was only a—Christmas gift to Pegeen's cousins, the Flahertys. It was all the Christmas dinner they were likely to have. Mama, you should have seen how they have to live. Down in that desperate hole in the ground, and the children blue with—"

"Now, Emily," her mother said, "we do our best by Pegeen. She is one of us in this household, but we cannot feed all of Ireland. We do what we can, but we cannot change the world, or even the city of New York. And I'm sure Mamie and her family feel the same."

I couldn't see Mamie's face. Obediently she'd gone over to sit in front of the fire, keeping clear of this conversation.

"But of course you are right, Emily," Mrs. Dunlap said. "Nobody likes to take charity, and Pegeen is too proud to ask for it, even for her own family. We will say no more about it."

They'd probably said too much, because Pegeen was there in the door. The last time I'd seen her, she'd about run me down with a tea tray. Now she didn't look so big. Her apron was extra starchy today, and so was her cap. She was carrying a tray again, with a cake on it and a jug with glasses. The room filled with the smell of spice and cider.

Her eyes were down. I thought she was good looking, but I didn't know. She was a type you don't see anymore. Of all of them, she looked the most like a girl in an old picture.

Mrs. Dunlap jumped. "Pegeen! Just bring in those refreshments. I expect Mr. Dunlap home directly."

Nobody spoke till Pegeen went away again. Emily was walking up and down in front of the fire, switching her bustle around. "And where is Tyler, if one may ask?" she said over Mamie's head.

"I believe he is paying a Christmas Day call," Mrs. Dunlap said. "But I expect him home . . . directly."

Emily sighed one of her mother's own sighs. "I daresay he's at the Ebersoles' this minute, following Consuelo around like a sheep."

"As to that, I couldn't say." Mrs. Dunlap stared meaningfully at the back of Mamie's head, but it didn't slow down Emily.

"The trouble with my brother is—"

But Mamie put up her hand to Emily. "You will want Tyler to be happy," she said in her musical voice. "We all do. Shall we light the candles on the tree?"

They'd lighted only a few before the front door banged open, sending a blast of cold air through the house. It sounded like a struggle had broken out in the entryway. A man's voice rang out.

"Explain yourself, sir! What is the meaning of this confounded intrusion?"

Mrs. Dunlap clutched the arm of her chair.

"Haw haw," came another voice. "That is to say—Ho ho."

Emily had turned from the tree with wide eyes. At the parlor door an amazing sight appeared.

A man, Mr. Dunlap, stepped into the room. He seemed to have lost his hat, but he was wearing a big black coat with a fur collar. He had a mustache on him like a walrus, and he was bald as an egg. He was holding somebody else by the back of the neck. It seemed to be Santa Claus. A very thin Santa Claus with a cotton beard beginning to slip and a beat-up old red Santa Claus suit with a cap that flopped down in front.

Mr. Dunlap stared around the room, seeing everybody but us. To his wife he said in a booming voice, "See here, Leonore, this vagrant I discovered trying to gain entry!"

"Oh, Jeremiah," she said, "turn him loose at once. It is Santa Claus himself. This is Christmas Day, and I wonder it could have escaped your notice. Surely the *Sun* newspaper has mentioned it."

"Christmas Day, you say?" Santa Claus was practically turning in the air, because Mr. Dunlap had a good grip on his collar and was holding him high. "By George, so it is!"

Luke's eyes were bugging out. He was really taking all this in.

Santa Claus got free and was pulling off his beard and climbing out of his costume. Inside was this young guy in a neat black suit, and he had the beginnings of his dad's mustache. It was Tyler, grinning.

"Men," Emily said to Mamie. "They never grow up."

I don't know how long we stood there, watching the Dunlaps and Mamie celebrate the Christmas of 1887. I think my knees locked, and so did Luke's, but we didn't miss anything. When they got the candles lighted on the tree, there was kind of a magic in the room. Tyler put another scoop of coal on the fire.

The party shifted over to the tree when they began opening their presents. There weren't many, and a lot of them were homemade. Emily had stitched up something called a corset cover for Mamie, who turned pink and hid her face from Tyler when she saw what it was.

Pretty soon the floor was full of tissue paper, and they were laughing at everything.

They sang "Good King Wenceslas" and "I Heard the Bells on Christmas Day." Mr. Dunlap boomed. Tyler tried to sing harmony. Mamie's voice came out truest. It was great. It was like having another family in another time. Then, after all the other presents were opened, Mr. Dunlap reached into the tree and felt around on the branches. He pulled out a little velvet box.

"I believe this has your name on it, Leonore."

"Surely not," Mrs. Dunlap said, putting out her hand.

She opened the box and took out a little pin in the shape of a bar. From here it looked like pearls and emeralds. There was a flash of green. She looked up at Mr. Dunlap like she'd kiss him if the children weren't here. Then she pinned it across her collar.

"It is exquisite," she said.

"Mr. Tiffany assisted me in selecting the design," Mr. Dunlap roared softly.

"You require no assistance, Jeremiah. Your taste is impeccable."

They scrambled around then, swaying their bustles, picking up all the tissue paper to save. Tyler rose to his feet.

Though he was dressed kind of like an undertaker, he was a good-looking guy. Kind of a pre-preppie and maybe fairly tall for his generation. He cleared his voice and said, "I have a gift for us all." He looked around at everybody. "For you, too, Mamie," he added.

All afternoon Emily had been shifting around so Tyler was next to Mamie. But they kept drifting apart.

"We are all invited to a New Year's Eve Ball," he said, running a finger around his tall collar. "We are all invited to welcome in 1888 at a ball to be held at the Ebersole residence."

Mrs. Dunlap let out a little screech.

"Mr. and Mrs. Ebersole request the pleasure of our company. And Miss Ebersole, of course. It's in honor of their houseguest, His Grace, the duke of Castleberry, from England."

Mrs. Dunlap stared around wildly. "A duke! The Ebersoles! What in heaven's name shall I wear?"

"Never mind, Leonore," Mr. Dunlap rumbled. "You can wear whatever you have. They wouldn't have seen it. By George, we are coming up in the world!"

I thought Tyler's news would send Emily into orbit. She went a little pale and glanced at Mamie. But then Emily's eyes narrowed, and she smiled, slightly.

From the door somebody spoke, and we all turned around.

"Christmas dinner is served, Mrs. Dunlap," Pegeen said. Her eyes were cast down as usual, but she looked up once, quick. At Tyler. Then she melted away.

They all started out the door, and Mamie said she better be getting home. Her family would wonder what on earth had become of her. But Emily held her back. It was only the two of them in the room with us.

"It will be a triumph," Emily said, squeezing Mamie's hand, "that New Year's Eve ball."

"I wouldn't think of going," Mamie murmured.

"Oh, Mamie, when *will* you start asserting yourself? You would outshine the vulgar Consuelo Ebersole in the midst of that vulgar ballroom in their vulgar mansion. The scales would fall from Tyler's eyes and he would see that you are worth any number of Consuelos!"

"Oh, Emily."

"After all, Mamie, you are in love with Tyler, are you not?"

Mamie gave her a long look. "Emily, I'm not sure where what you want for me ends and what I want for me begins."

Emily blinked. "Don't be so intellectual, Mamie. Men don't like it."

Then they both swept out of the room, leaving me and Luke alone. We stood there, all those Christmases ago.

"Time to get back," Luke said, "if we can."

Ten

The fire burned low, and the Christmas-tree candles had all guttered out. We could hear the Dunlaps on the floor below, settling down to their dinner. It was time to go.

"How?" I said.

"I don't know," Luke said, "but we can't keep doing this if we can't get back."

A real wintertime chill went through me. Luke was giving everything thought. I like to be in charge of us, but I sure couldn't see what the next move was.

"I think doors are part of it," he said, "if you happen to be inside at the time."

Doors?

"I remember one time back home . . . but that might not have anything to do with it."

"What about back home, Luke? You mean California?"

He nodded. "I was real little at the time. Once I got up in the night, one of those times when you all thought I was walking in my sleep. But I'd heard something, so I got up to check it out. I went downstairs, and when I opened the door to the utility room, it was a real sunny day down there, and I saw an Indian lady."

"A what? How did you know she was an Indian?"

"Beads and buckskin, a few feathers, moccasins. She was an Indian, all right. She had a baby strapped on her back."

"What was she doing? Her laundry?"

Luke gave me an impatient look. "She was just walking. She walked across the utility room, except the floor was rocks and brush. Then she went on through the wall. I think there must have been an Indian trail through there at one time."

"Luke—"

"I wasn't asleep," he said. "No way. That real door to the utility room kind of lined up with a door in my mind. I was small. I didn't know how I did it. I probably thought it was just a game, not something I was going to need to use someday. It's true, Chad."

"I believe you. That's what worries me."

The doors to the front parlor were open. It was dim, but it was 1887 in there too. Luke pointed at the ceiling. Out in the hall I said, "If we're going upstairs, we could take the elevator." It was right there, and it kind of fascinated me. You could see the cables reaching up into the house above it.

"We better not," he said. "They might hear it down there."

"They won't hear it. They're all at the dinner table, talking. And they're keeping the servants busy."

But Luke hung back like he didn't have a good feeling about the elevator. I wasn't sure how to work the thing but figured it had to be fairly simple. Luke got in with me. He wasn't happy about it even though you could see out through the bars. I didn't see what his problem was. He hadn't minded that boxy little private elevator in Old Man Pendleton's apartment.

I pulled the doors shut and reached for a wooden-handled lever, easing it up. We jolted. I pulled farther back, and we began to rise, clanking a little. The front hall fell away under us, and we climbed up the stripes of the wallpaper. It seemed safe enough. This cage was really built to last. Luke was holding his breath.

"Let's get out on the second floor," he said.

I had to play around with the lever. If you didn't line up the cage with the floor exactly, the doors wouldn't open, but we made it. When we stepped out, a door was directly in front of us.

"I told you Emily's room was right there," Luke said.

I stood there while he thought. He figured if we somehow got in the right frame of mind and burst through that door, it might be the twentieth century on the other side. It would be Mom and Dad's dressing rooms maybe. Now I was ready to get back, really ready.

Luke spit on his hands. In a leap he went for the door, grabbed the knob, and we were both through it.

He was right about one thing. It was Emily's room. But it was still 1887 in here too. A little lamp burned in the corner. Now I wasn't in such a big hurry because you could sense Emily here.

A picture of Tyler stood on her table, a stiff shot of

him in a hat, trying to look older. She had a little white
bed with a satin quilt on it and a lot of books around.
The one on her table was *Snow-Bound* by John Green-
leaf Whittier.

Luke was taking everything in. He ran his hand over
the copy of *Snow-Bound.* He turned the heavy cover
over, and Emily had written her name in brown ink on
the first page. It was the first time I'd seen her signa-
ture. I wanted to run my hand over it.

"It's a lot to figure," Luke said quietly.

"What?"

"Well, we're here, aren't we? We can feel the temperature and smell the smells. We can open doors and . . .
run the elevator. I can open the cover of this book, and
yet I wonder if it's enough."

He turned, too quiet for an ordinary kid, and looked
at the far wall of the room. It was mostly toys that Emily
had saved from when she was younger, big dolls with
china heads and shoes that buttoned up like hers. And a
hobbyhorse covered with authentic horsehair. The
mane was all there, and the bridle was in good condition.

"It's not in the attic yet." He remembered how we'd
seen it up there forty years later in 1928, falling apart. I
wanted to stay right here before anything had started
falling apart. I could feel the room urging me to stay.

But I followed Luke back out into the hall. We could
see into the front bedroom, and it was 1887 all the way
through the lace curtains of the front window. Down at

the other end it was dark by Tyler's door. I was beginning to worry. What if we used up all the doors and never got anywhere? But Luke just said, "Let's go," and we went. We got slower down by Tyler's door. I remembered the last time: the killer cold, the snow deep on his windowsill, that bad empty feeling. My hand gripped Luke's shoulder, but his hand was going for the knob. We didn't try barreling through this time. Luke turned the knob slow and easy. The door unlatched. He gave it a push, but we held our ground.

Sunshine hit us, and I was blind as a bat for a minute. Everything looked like a photo negative. I could see the blood vessels in my eyeballs darting around like minnows. It was Heidi's room now, with the summer sunlight falling in through her vertical blinds onto wall-to-wall carpeting. The big old dark wood door Luke had just pushed open was enameled white with a modern knob.

"Nice work," I muttered to him, but he shrugged it off.

This door business reminded me of doing math problems. Sometimes they work out. Sometimes you're back where you started.

Through the crack in the door Luke and I both saw a quick movement in the room, like a big bird fluttering. He nudged the door farther open. Heidi's bed was a jumble with a big lump in the middle of it. The lump moved.

We were keeping our distance when this head

appeared. It was Heidi, though I had to look twice to recognize her. Her hair was on end, but pretty much back to its real color. She'd given herself a major shampoo, and the black stuff had washed out. Heidi looked washed out herself. She had her sheet pulled up. You could see bare shoulders, but she was wearing something. I couldn't tell what.

"Hey, Heidi, you sick or something?"

"Me?" She blinked. ". . . No." But her mind was way off somewhere.

"Where's Jocelyn?"

"Who? Oh. They're all at the Frick Museum, or someplace. Her mom, our mom, Jocelyn. They've got all these sightseeing things to do. Or they're looking at apartments. Or shopping. It's endless. I came home. My feet hurt."

Heidi was shrinking behind her sheet. She was just eyes and hair, but everything you could see was her natural color. I turned Luke around, and we left. But as I pulled the door shut behind us, I noticed something different about her room. All her bookshelves were empty. "Boy, they go through a lot of phases in high school, don't they?" I said to Luke.

He just shrugged. "I'll tell you one thing. She wasn't napping."

I pointed out that she was in bed in the middle of the afternoon, blinking.

"She jumped into bed when the door opened. I saw

her," he said. "She'd been trying on clothes, or something."

"What's she up to, Luke? She's pulled back from her new Jocelyn image. She's dumped all her romance books. She's up to something. What?"

He didn't know, and I didn't get anything more out of him until that night. Heidi didn't come down to dinner, so it was just the four of us. We ordered in, New York style: cold sesame noodles and moo shu pork with chasers of celery tonic and for dessert a Carvel ice-cream cake in the shape of a firecracker.

After dinner Luke and I sent Mom and Dad out to sit on the stoop for some evening air while we loaded the dishwasher. When we had the kitchen to ourselves, Luke wandered over to the window that looked up to Seventy-third Street. You could see the lower halves of people walking along the sidewalk. Mom and Dad had taken Al out with them. She was sitting there on the concrete, monitoring everybody who went by, keeping an eye out for Dobermans.

As I set the dishwasher on the presoak cycle, Luke said, "Remember last night, Chad? When we walked up to Seventy-ninth Street and saw the Ebersoles' mansion where that high-rise is now?" He was really looking his dreamiest. "Did you notice there was snow around the house and they were having a party?"

"Maybe."

"I think it was the New Year's Eve ball that Tyler told us about. The one the Ebersoles were giving for His

Grace, the duke of Castleberry, England. We should go to it."

We?

"Emily's going," he said, watching me. I'd strolled over to the window with him. And I was thinking of Emily at the Ebersoles' ball, not like in my dream, but like it really was.

"Also," Luke said, "we might pick up some clues about why we keep slipping into their world and why they keep nagging at our dreams."

We both gazed out the window past a small mountain of Meaningful Moments at Honey Brook High and every published copy of Pep Squadders in Love, overflowing our garbage can.

"How could we?" I said. "This afternoon it was Christmas day for the Dunlaps. So how could last night be New Year's Eve at the Ebersoles? You've got your dates mixed up, Luke."

But he didn't think so. "I doubt if it works like that. The past isn't like a schoolday where everything happens on the same schedule, year in, year out. I think the Ebersoles' New Year's Eve ball is going on right now, Chad. I really feel it happening, and I think we could drop in on it later, if we play our cards right."

"I don't know." But I could hear music, faintly, in my head. Waltz music.

"We'll go to bed around the regular time," Luke said. "Let Mom and Dad settle down, and then I'll meet you out in the hall. Dress warm. If it works, it'll be winter."

We stood at the kitchen window while evening crept up the houses across the street. Al was just a small champagne-colored shape out there on the sidewalk, and you couldn't read any of the titles on the heap of romance books.

"I wonder why Heidi pitched out all her books."

"Oh, well, that part's easy." Luke reached down to scratch under his sock. "Girls only read romance books when they aren't having one."

"One what?"

"A romance."

"You mean to tell me she's been getting calls from California? You mean—Thor Desmond lives?"

"I wouldn't go that far," he said.

Eleven

When I met Luke out in the hall, I was wearing two Gant sweaters over a polo and my Windbreaker. He was layered, too, and it gave him a whole new shape. We waited at the stairs, listening to the house.

"Now what?"

"We ought to check on Heidi," he said.

We crept down to her floor. It was dark, but we knew the way. Mom and Dad had closed their door half an hour ago. Light came from under Heidi's. We went in. Maverick stared down at us from the wall, but she wasn't around. Luke headed for her bathroom. We slipped in there and shut the door behind us. I really don't like the idea that somebody can come up behind you.

Every bulb was on, and her hair dryer was still warm. Steam lingered on her mirror. Luke went through the wastebasket. It was mostly Kleenex. But she'd thrown out her black lip-gloss and three empty containers of black tinting mousse and those nuts-and-bolts earrings. He seemed to see all this as clues. Then he turned back to the bedroom door.

"Help me concentrate, Chad," he said as his little hand closed over the knob. "Make your mind like it was back when you were about three years old, before it got all cluttered up."

"Luke, when I was three, my mind was already cluttered up. All day long I kept thinking about Fisher-Price toys."

"Well, then, don't think about anything, and I'll see what I can do." His forehead rested against the door. He pushed it open, and it was Tyler's room in there. A minute before, it had been Heidi's. Now it wasn't. A light snow hit the black panes of Tyler's window. A lamp glowed by his brass bed. The chamber pot lurked under it.

"Bingo," Luke said.

We walked in, and the glare from Heidi's bathroom faded out behind us. I looked around, and the bathroom door was now a smooth stretch of wall with ivy leaves in the paper and a pennant reading YALE.

"Bingo," I muttered, though my mouth was really dry.

We walked to the stairwell where the elevator cables hung down. Music floated up, an accordion wheezing sound from the kitchen below. You could hear glasses clinking and feet tapping and laughter coming from the basement.

"The servants," Luke said, "Pegeen and the others. It's New Year's Eve for them too."

Then we were out of the house and walking, that evening of December 31, 1887, leaning into the snowy wind. When we turned up Fifth Avenue, the world was blue with the light of the gas lamps. On our left closed carriages headed uptown to the Ebersoles' ball.

The mansion was like we'd seen it before, blazing with light. On the curving drive footmen handed down ladies and gentlemen. We crossed Seventy-ninth Street, dodging horses, and the scene got realer. We were in the snowy shrubbery, keeping clear of the people and the swinging carriage doors. Up by the front entrance it was an amazing scene: men in tall top hats and women in big furs and diamonds. The carpet stretching down the marble steps was blood red.

"How do we get inside?" I said, whispering for no reason. Next to this crowd Luke looked incredible in his puffy jacket and three little golf shirts. He was watching to find out how it all worked.

The footmen at the front door wore satin knee britches and silk stockings, but they were way over six feet high. Their white-gloved hands could separate your head from your body. These guys were obviously hired to keep out the uninvited.

"They can't see you, but you've got to deal with the doors," Luke said. "Get in behind a man. It's ladies first, and then the men go in. So go, and keep close." I picked a big gent with a billowing coat. The footmen swung the doors extra wide, and I went in on his heels. Luke came in with the next couple.

My dream was nothing compared to the real Ebersole mansion. The place was lots bigger and finer, like a museum. They should never have torn it down. The hall at the top of the first flight was three stories high, with fountains. We hugged the walls to keep out of the traffic pattern. It was like a public place, and I wondered if I'd ever find Emily. At the top of the stairs the Ebersoles were greeting their guests.

Luke and I were behind a big marble urn, a stone's throw from Mrs. Ebersole. She was at the top of the stairs where everybody could see her. The main diamond in her tiara was the size of a headlight. She carried a big ostrich-feather fan and wore diamond rings over her gloves.

"His Grace, the duke of Castleberry," she said to everybody. The line of people waiting to see a duke was backed up all the way down to the front door. His Grace was as tall as a footman, and he wore a fine tailcoat. He had a monocle wedged over his right eye, and he put out his hand and said, "Howjadew" to everybody, speaking over their heads.

"He's bored out of his skull," Luke said.

Next to the duke was somebody so short, I nearly missed her. She was a squat girl, shaped like a teapot. Her pink dress had a lot of bows at the top of it. Big diamonds pulled her ears down. Some feathers were in her hair to make her look taller, and she was carrying a small bouquet of yellow flowers that clashed with her dress.

"Consuelo," Luke said. But she was really different from my dream. Her dad stood next to her, and she looked a lot like him. Between the two of them they had at least five chins. Cigars stuck up from Mr. Ebersole's coat pocket, and he looked like he could use one. Luke and I moved on. More stairs curved up, and we heard music, waltzes, mingling in the air with the perfume and cigar smoke.

By walking along walls and around footmen we came to the ballroom, and it was sensational. Rows of crystal chandeliers multiplied in the mirrors. A lot of people sat around the walls in gold chairs, and the floor was full of twirling dancers. We had less room to maneuver in here, but there were marble columns surrounded by gardenia plants as tall as trees. You could get in there without being stepped on. Once we were settled in, I could have watched all night.

The music was old-fashioned, but good. I had my eyes peeled for Emily, but unless she waltzed by, I'd probably miss her. Big doors opened behind us. All the Ebersoles and the duke of Castleberry came in. Consuelo gazed around the room, but she was too short to see much. She parked her bouquet under her arm and consulted the dance program that hung from her wrist.

"Miss Ebersole, I don't suppose yew would care to dawnce," the Duke said over her head.

Consuelo squinted at her program, red in the face. "I had thought to be promised to another partner for this dance," she said, "but all right. I mean, I should be charmed."

His Grace gave Consuelo his gloved hand. She

lurched forward, and her eyes bulged. I personally
think her mother gave her a shove.

"She'd rather be dancing with Tyler," Luke said.

As they waltzed away, Consuelo kept peering around
the duke's shoulder, looking for someone. Then the
lights dimmed. The orchestra struck up "Auld Lang
Syne," and rose petals started falling from the ceiling. It
was midnight. The crowds roared and horns blew, wel-
coming in 1888. People kissed each other. The duke
bent over Consuelo's plump little glove and planted a
dry kiss on her knuckles. Still, she was looking high and
low through the rose petals, for Tyler.

Luke and I hung on our pillar while the orchestra
played something that could have been a polka. Then
they were back to waltzes. We watched the dancers
moving in a big wheel around the ballroom floor.

Consuelo went around once with the duke, but there
were plenty of guys, all black and white like penguins,
cutting in to dance with an heiress. Though I almost
missed them, Mr. and Mrs. Dunlap went by. They were
about the best dancers, moving together like one per-
son. There was a flash of green up by Mrs. Dunlap's
throat. She looked as good as any of the older ladies in
the room, and I was proud of her.

Then I saw Emily. Her dress was white, high necked
because she was still young. No diamonds, of course.
Simpler than the others, and the prettiest girl in the
room. She whirled by, and her hair shimmered over her
shoulders. I thought she looked at me, or through me.

But anyway, she caught my eye even if I didn't catch hers.

She was smiling, and the program danced at her wrist. She was in the arms of the duke of Castleberry, and he wasn't bored now. His monocle was practically sending out sparks. All I wanted was to see her again, when she made the round and waltzed past our pillar. My guard was down, and I was wedged in between a marble column and a gardenia tree. Luke was there at my elbow, peering through the glossy leaves. He grabbed my arm.

"What?"

But he didn't answer. He just pointed. At first I saw Tyler, taller than the rest. He was waltzing our way. Luke's grip tightened. They were playing "The Beautiful Blue Danube," and here came Tyler. I only had a hint of the girl in his arms—the top of her head just above his shoulder, the sweep of her lacy skirts across the polished floor.

Luke was cutting off my circulation. "Luke, what?"

Tyler was turning now, holding his partner like precious cargo. Then we saw her. And she saw us. It was Heidi.

I nearly fell out of my gardenia tree. It was Heidi, wearing an ivory-colored lace dress, cut low, and high gloves. She had as much hair as any of them, and she'd swept it way up high on her head and sprayed it into shape, or something. Anyway, it fitted in. *She* fitted in. I couldn't believe this. Heidi, for Pete's sake.

Tyler turned her, but now she was turning back. Four hundred people in the room, but she was the only one who could see us. Her eyes fixed on mine and widened. Her hand closed tight on Tyler's shoulder. Then she spotted Luke. She stumbled once and then got a grip on herself. Tyler swept her up and away, and they were swallowed by the crowd.

"I didn't see that," I said. "I think I'm hallucinating, and I definitely didn't see that."

"You did too," Luke said. "I had a hunch about Heidi."

"Luke, she's really here. They can *see* her. Tyler can. He's dancing with her. She's *visible*. How did she do that?"

He shrugged. "I'm only—"

"I know. I know. You're only eight."

I was sweating through my layered clothes, and everybody around us was realer than we were. The room was heating up, and I had to see Heidi again to believe her. My head was whirling. I wasn't even looking for Emily.

"This can't be," I said to Luke, whispering now because who knew? "For one thing, where did she get that outfit?"

"Out of the trunk in the attic," he said. "She was up to something even then. I figured we could get to this party by going through her bathroom. She's been getting ready for this."

"How did we get here by going through her bathroom? What did that have to do with it?"

"I think Heidi sort of blazed a trail, and we came in
on it."

"Wait a minute, Luke. It's one thing for you and me
to . . . visit the past. But Heidi? She's never been farther than the mall. And remember her in Mom's Taurus? Heidi can't even *drive*, and she can do this? And
why? What's she doing here anyway?"

He muttered something.

"What?"

"Changing history," he said.

"What does that mean?"

"I'm not sure," he said, "but I think that's what's
happening."

They were coming around again, and I wasn't worried that Tyler could see us. He couldn't take his eyes off
Heidi. They negotiated a graceful turn in front of us,
and Heidi broke out of his arms. I was still having a lot of
trouble believing her. Her lips were pink now, not
black, and shaped just right. The dress gave her a figure
I didn't know she had. She was possibly the second
prettiest girl in this room. She sure knocked Consuelo
out of the ballpark, even though Heidi was about a
hundred million dollars poorer and hadn't been born
yet.

Right in front of us she turned back to Tyler and
spoke in an entirely new voice. "Oh, Tyler, I declare
you have, like, danced me off my feet. That's our ninth

waltz. Give me a break—I mean, I must withdraw and catch my breath."

He wouldn't let go of her hand. "But, darling," he said, "they'll be serving a collation directly. You must let me take you into the supper room."

"Oh, I shall return by, you know, then." Heidi pulled free, still graceful, and waved him away. He went, but he looked sad. Then she whipped around to face a potted gardenia tree—me and Luke.

"Can't I go *any*where without you two on my case?"

She was trying to talk without moving her lips, so it wouldn't look like she was having a conversation with a gardenia tree. "What are you two doing here anyway?" Amazingly, she had a little paper fan in her hand, a party favor maybe. She snapped it open with a sharp report and appeared to be fanning herself here by the pillar.

"Hey, Heidi, how did you learn to handle a fan?"

"Dame Barbara Cartland," she said behind it.

"Where is she?" I looked around the ballroom.

Heidi sighed. "She's a *writer*. She writes about all this." Heidi waved her fan around the crowds. "This isn't Honeybrook High, you know. This is something else." She was fanning up a storm. "And listen, I've got to get out of here, like now."

"How'd you get here?"

Her eyes darted around. "I came with Tyler. At least I followed him. And when I got here, people could see me, and I made real sure Tyler did."

"How did you get . . . visible?"

"Well, I usually get what I want," she said. Which is true. "And, I don't know, but I think the dress helped. It's of the period." She took a deep breath which really showed off the top part of her dress. Actually, she really did look a lot like the picture on the cover of one of those historical romances. She'd really outgrown Pep Squadders in Love.

"Dresses and doors," Luke mumbled beside us.

"But I've got to get out of here," Heidi said. "Tyler's . . . great, but he's asking me a whole lot of questions I can't answer. He wants to know where I *live.* And I live in his *room.* Or he lives in mine. It's confusing. Every time I come through that bathroom door of mine, I don't know *what* to expect. Walk me to the entrance of this place. I can't even tell where it is."

"We have to be careful," Luke said. "People can't see me and Chad, and they'll walk all over us."

"Well, stay right behind me and, like, steer me," Heidi said. "And watch the train. It's tricky."

Heidi swept up her train and moved out. The crowds parted, and we walked in step behind her. She handled it really well. Some of the guys bowed to her, and she gave them little nods back and did some business with her fan. I looked back once, hoping for another glimpse of Emily, but I didn't see her.

When we got down to the big hall with the fountains, people were beginning to leave. Ladies were draping their furs around their shoulders. The front doors were in sight.

"Take it easy, Heidi," I said because she was putting on some speed now. "Don't panic."

The footmen opened both doors, and the three of us were almost out of there. Luke was practically clinging to my back. A voice rang out behind us. Tyler's. "No, darling, don't go!" I looked back to see him racing down the stairs. His shiny leather shoes were a black blur against the white marble. He elbowed people out of the way and looked straight through Luke and me to Heidi. "Darling, you can't leave!"

She looked back, and her eyes were huge. Lifting her skirts, she blasted off through the doors and outdistanced us all. Luke and I got out of Tyler's way. Then we followed him outside. A cold wind hit us. Heidi was gone, swallowed up by the darkness. Tyler stood there, and his shoulders slumped.

But something was lying on the red-carpeted step, something that made no sense to him. We watched him reach down and pick it up. He turned it in his hand, every direction, but he didn't know what to make of it. Confused and discouraged, he tossed it aside into the shrubbery. It was one of Heidi's sneakers. A Reebok.

By then I thought we'd had about enough excitement for one night, even New Year's Eve. But the doors opened behind us, and you could feel the heat of the house and the party. We all three turned around.

Consuelo stood there with a face pinker than her

dress. Her mouth worked, and the diamonds vibrated in her ears. She was like a little round hornet, very mad.

"Tyler Dunlap! You have shamed me in my own house and before everybody who counts and a member of the English peerage." People were coming out the door—witnesses. But Consuelo didn't care. "Tyler, you are treacherous and faithless." Her voice jumped up an octave. "And you have made a fool of me with the first pretty face to come your way!"

From behind her back she whipped out her bouquet of yellow flowers, crocuses. "And you can take back your weeds, you rotter!" She pitched the bouquet at him, and he was so surprised, he caught it.

She turned on her heel. The footmen threw open the doors, and she stamped inside. Tyler stood there holding his own bouquet. If you looked hard, you could see the little gold paper letters on the long ribbon:

WITH RESPECTFUL AFFECTION

T.D.

Twelve

We made it home through the snowy early morning of New Year's Day, 1888. And when we got inside our own door, we were back to normal. Al was sitting on her scooper in the twentieth-century hallway waiting up for us. The central air-conditioning of a June night hummed in the background. Luke was really beat, and I was pretty droopy myself. Time travel can hit you harder than jet lag. I just made it out of my clothes and into bed. And, you guessed it, I dreamed.

I dreamed about us, just our family, the way we were in California. We were home again in the Rio Bravo subdivision where it's always fair weather. There weren't any shadows anywhere and a minimum of doors. And no history. We were in the family room, in full color. It was great to be back.

But all dreams are strange. In this one Dad was Alan Thicke from *Growing Pains*. And Mom looked almost exactly like the mom on *The Wonder Years*. Dad was using a rug for a putting green though in real life he doesn't even play golf. Mom was wearing an apron, which she hardly ever does. Luke was there, except he looked like Chip used to on *Kate & Allie*. Though I couldn't see myself, I was hoping to be a young Kirk

Cameron. Everybody had very white teeth and terrific tans.

Heidi breezed into the dream, Heidi-before-New-York in one of her pastel Esprit outfits. Except she was Stephanie from the *Newhart* show. "Hey, Mom," she said in her own voice, "I'm due over at Melissa's like ten minutes ago."

Mom reached into her apron pocket and lobbed a set of keys to Heidi, who plucked them out of the air. She walked straight across the dream and out the door.

"Hey, Heidi," I yelled after her, "you don't have your license. You can't even find reverse!"

And this must have been a punch line because the laugh track went crazy. We were definitely a sitcom. If you looked close, you could see the shape of the screen around the edges of the dream.

Alan Thicke looked up from his putting green, and Dad said, "It's like California out there this morning. What I've got in mind is a real family outing, all five of us. It'll be great."

"But, Dad," I said, "Heidi's not here. Didn't you see her go?" But he didn't hear me. Lots of times in dreams, you're yelling at people, and they can't hear you. Now we were cutting away for a commercial.

"Don't go away," Mom said, holding up a popular brand of foaming cleanser. "We'll be right back." She smiled into the camera. Al whined once, and the screen went dark.

Then she whined again. I was awake now, up in my

New York room with the light sliding in the windows. Al was there by the door. Her head was on one side with a floppy ear almost over one bulgy eye. She whined again because she likes to see us all up and moving around early.

I climbed out of bed, not too rested, not too sure what was happening. When I was showered and dressed, I could smell coffee drifting up through the house, so maybe I hadn't missed breakfast. Down a flight I met Luke. He was just sitting there on the stairs, waiting for me. I nearly kicked him in the head before I saw him there.

"I must have overslept. Come on, let's grab some breakfast."

But he wasn't budging. His chin was in his fists, and his elbows were on his little knobby knees, and something was wrong.

"We've got a problem," he said. "Heidi."

"What about her?"

"She's not here. She wasn't downstairs having breakfast with Mom and Dad. So I came up to her room. I thought maybe she was sleeping in, but then I thought maybe she wasn't." He looked up at me with big worried eyes. "She wasn't."

"You mean—"

"She never came home last night. I've checked everywhere, Chad. She never made it . . . back."

"Wait a minute—"

"And how are we going to explain this to Mom and

Dad?" He ground his fists into his chin. "They're still down there at the table."

My mind went blank but only for a moment. We didn't have much time. "We'll have to tell them something."

"It won't be the truth," Luke said sadly.

And of course he had a point. We couldn't quite tell Mom and Dad that Heidi got caught in a time warp, wearing a ball gown and one Reebok, and she was tied up somewhere between now and 1888. In the cold light of day I had a little problem with this myself. Except it was true.

"But if we don't tell them something," Luke said, "what are they going to do?"

"Get real upset and call the cops."

Luke nodded, way ahead of me as usual. "And what good will that do? They'll all think we know something we aren't telling, and they'll be right."

"Jocelyn," I said, already at the end of my rope. "We can say Heidi was up early on the phone with Jocelyn. And they . . . decided to spend the day together."

"Where?" Luke said into his fists.

"Do I know?"

"You better."

"Okay, they went to the Botanical Gardens, in the Bronx."

Luke looked up and blinked. "Jocelyn and Heidi? That's a big lie, Chad, and it'll get bigger." He sighed and stood up slow like a little old man. "Come on, we better get downstairs. I'll think of something."

Mom and Dad were down there, and actually he has a lot better build than Alan Thicke. The table was heaped with food: fruit, eggs, a pile of bagels, a mound of cream cheese. We looked like a deli. "What's happening?" I said.

"It's Sunday." Dad looked up from a *New York Times.* "We've been through this with Luke. Are you two losing track of time?"

Not a bad way to put it.

Dad started sliding food our way, and Mom poured us some juice. I didn't have any appetite. Heidi can be pretty annoying at times, but I'd have felt a lot better if she was here with us. There was this hole where Heidi should be. Luke was picking the raisins out of a bagel and keeping a low profile.

"You guys look a little down," Dad said. "Have you looked outside? It's like California out there this morning. What I've got in mind is a real family outing, all five of us. It'll be great."

Mom went over to the foot of the stairs. She was just about to call Heidi down to breakfast.

"Mom," Luke said. He had all the raisins out of his bagel in a neat pile on the plate. "Heidi's not coming down."

"That girl," Mom said. "She isn't sick, is she? I better go up and—"

"No, Mom," he said. "She's . . . fine. It's her hair."

We were all listening to him now, intently.

"Oh, no, Luke, don't tell me." Mom clutched her forehead. "That black dye job was bad enough. Don't tell me she's cut it all off like Jocelyn's. If she's chopped off all her lovely hair, it'll break my heart."

"Be calm, Mom," he said. "Heidi's going to wash all that black glop out of her hair, and get back to . . . normal. But it'll take her all day. She wants it to be kind of a surprise."

It was amazingly convincing. I almost believed it myself.

"So we better just kind of . . . leave her alone today."

Dad sighed.

As we left the house, he yelled up the stairs, "We're going now, honey. We'll leave Al to keep you company." But finally we were out of there, and I have to say it was the longest Sunday I've ever lived through.

The four of us took the subway down to the South Street Seaport, looked it over, and had a late lunch at Wok & Roll on Pier 17. Then we cabbed back up to the Forty-second Street pier and took the three-hour Circle Line cruise around Manhattan. We were tourists all day, and Luke and I walked through the whole experience like two androids.

We floated down the Hudson, past Battery Park City and the World Trade Center towers and the Statue of Liberty. There were these great views, and Mom and

Dad took a lot of pictures. Luke and I sat on a bench, trying not to huddle.

Under the Brooklyn Bridge he said in a small voice, "What if she's gone for good, Chad? Forever and ever. What then?"

And I really didn't know.

The sun was setting into Central Park by the time we climbed up out of the Sixty-eighth Street subway. We were on the home stretch now, and I dreaded getting there. Luke and I trudged along, dropping back behind Mom and Dad. He was holding my hand, which he doesn't do much anymore.

"Things look bad, Chad," he said, quietly. "How are we ever going to help Emily and Tyler when we can't even keep track of Heidi? It's like somebody pulled the plug, and they've all gone down the drain. I'm pretty discouraged."

I thought he was going to break down and start bawling. I thought we both might. When we turned into Seventy-third Street, his lower lip was out. When we followed Mom and Dad up the stoop, his chin was quivering. The whole situation was completely out of control.

"Dad," I said, figuring it was confession time, "I—"

But just as he put the key in the front door, it opened.

Heidi was standing there in her California jumpsuit in camouflage colors and her big blond California hair standing out from her head like a halo. It was Heidi. She blinked at us. "Where have all of you been?" she said, faintly.

Mom and Dad lit up at the sight of all that blond hair. Luke shot through between them, grabbed Heidi around the waist, and gave her a big hug. He sobbed once. I could have hugged her myself, and I also felt like punching her out.

Mom and Dad looked at all of us. "Why do I have the feeling," Mom said, "that there's something I don't know?"

Al was underfoot, trying to climb up all of us, and she looked like she was about to explode.

"Heidi," I said, "why haven't you taken Al for a walk?" I sort of barked this out.

"Who, me?" she said. "I just—"

"And, Dad," I said, "look at Luke. He's worn out. He got too much sun on that Circle Line. Put him to bed." And Luke was reaching up like he wanted Dad to pick him up, which he hasn't done since preschool. I was barking commands right and left. Mom gave me an inquisitive look.

"Come on, Heidi, we'll take Al for a walk together," I snapped. "Get her leash and her scooper. You're not too good to scoop." She was so surprised, she obeyed.

Then it was just me and Heidi, strolling together along Seventy-third Street and up Madison Avenue. She wasn't saying anything, but I'd caught her off guard. "Heidi, I've about had it with you. Luke and I thought you were gone for good."

"I don't know what you're talking about," she said, her eyes shifting away. "You all went off this morning and left me behind."

"Wrong, Heidi. You weren't there. You never came home last night."

"I wasn't out anywhere . . . last night," she said in a voice a complete stranger wouldn't have believed.

"For one thing, what did you do with the dress?" I said, quick.

"I put it back in the trunk. I mean, what dress?"

"Look, Heidi, last night you were back in time a hundred-plus years at the Ebersoles' ball. *Duke of Castleberry* ring a bell? I mean, fine. I didn't know you had it in you, but—"

"I'm so *sure*," Heidi hissed, but she was looking all around everywhere but at me. "I may have been reading too many of those Dame Barbara Cartland books. And I've been having, like, funny dreams."

"That was no dream, Heidi. I was *in* it."

She nudged me. "Okay, call it a nightmare."

"I'm serious, Heidi."

But I could feel her slipping out of my grasp. Al was in and out of the gutter, looking for just the right spot, so maybe she hadn't been about to explode after all.

"By the way," I said, "what do you hear from Thor Desmond?"

"Don't be a goober," Heidi said. "Those T.D. initials weren't Thor. They were Tyler Dun—"

She froze. We were at a stoplight anyway. There was

Sunday-night traffic all around us, and people in and out of delis. Heidi looked good, very up to date. You wouldn't have believed where she'd been last night, unless you'd been there. Guys looked at her as they went past us.

"When you're older, you'll understand, Chad."

I hate it when she gets mature with me.

"When you're in high school, you'll know stuff."

"Such as?"

"Like you've really got to be super normal, or people will think you're a total spaz. You just can't *be* different or be able to do anything that other people can't. I mean, if Melissa Schultz knew . . . let's just take this as an example. If Melissa knew I was having this intense relationship with—somebody. Like I was living in his same *room,* but he didn't exactly know I was there because he wasn't exactly—alive at the time. . . ."

"What would Melissa say?"

"She'd say I needed brain surgery. She'd tell everybody I was totally zeeked out."

"Heidi, if she'd think that, she's no friend."

"That's how it works in high school, Chad. Period." She pursed up her mouth to show how certain she was. Her lips had just enough gloss on them to give them a good shape, like at the ball.

"When did you first know Tyler was there, Heidi?"

She sighed. "The first night we got here. I dreamed him, but it was more like he dreamed me. Look, I'd just gotten off a plane. I'm like, what is this—jet lag? But it was Tyler."

We were crossing Madison Avenue by the Carlyle Hotel to come back down the other side. "I thought I could fight it," she said. "I'm not even *into* history. I got a C in it last semester. So when I met Jocelyn, I thought being like her would solve everything. I mean, she's so New Wave."

"You mean you thought that dyeing your hair would get Tyler off your case?"

She nodded. "I'd have tried anything. I'd have punked completely out. But maybe . . . the other thing is stronger."

"The other thing?"

". . . Like love," Heidi whispered.

We walked on awhile with Al bobbing along ahead of us. "It's cool," I told her. "When you get home, you can tell Melissa all about this great guy you met in New York."

"She'd want proof," Heidi said. "What am I supposed to do, show her an old tintype of Tyler in a collar and a *hat*?"

"Where'd you see a picture like that?"

"It's in my bathroom sometimes. It comes and goes. I think my bathroom was his sister's room. Who knows? That whole house is so Fang Castle I can't believe it. It's different for you and Luke. You sleep upstairs where nothing ever happens. I'm right down there in their flight path, or whatever."

We were walking slower, and Heidi was window-shopping with one eye. Old habits are hard to break. "Anyway, forget Melissa, okay? What am I going to do, tell her the only guy I met in the entire city of New York is a dead dude, and I'm crazy about him?"

But there was more I wanted to know.

"Listen, Heidi, where'd you go last night? You shot out of the Ebersoles' ball like a big bat, and you were heading for home. Where were you all night?"

But I'd pushed her too far. She was clamming up. "I . . . lost my way."

"It was only six blocks," I said, carefully.

"And it was cold. The wind went right through that dress. It's lace. I only had one shoe."

"What do you mean, you lost your way?"

"I don't want to think about it." She was really clamming up.

"Something happened, Heidi."

She nodded, slightly. "But I don't understand it. The farther I got from the Ebersoles, the darker it got, and colder. It was this nightmare, and I was running and running. When I got back to the house, I thought everything would be back to . . . now. But there was something wrong."

"With the house?"

"It was empty. Deserted. Nobody lived there. Nobody'd lived there for years. It was in some other time, not back in the Dunlaps' days, and not now. Sometime in between. And the house was ruined and dead and boarded up. And I didn't know what to do. I was in a time where I didn't know anybody."

"But you did something."

"The stoop was full of trash, and the front door was boarded up like the windows. But I kept yanking on the boards till they came loose." She remembered her hands and looked down at them. They were all scraped up.

"I got inside, and it was worse. Nobody could live in there. Just little creatures with claws or wings. Everybody was gone or dead or I don't know. I felt my way upstairs to my room. It was empty, too, and everything had fallen apart. I couldn't go on. Where was I supposed to go? I curled up on the floor and thought about dying. I thought everybody was dead, so why not me?"

"And when you woke up, you were in your room, and it was back to now."

"Like that," Heidi said.

"I wonder how you did it."

"Well, I really wanted to get back, and I usually get what I want." Which we already know. "And it was something else. I had to stay alive and—be me because there was something important I have to do. I heard it in the house. All last night I heard the house telling me what I have to do, but I don't know now. I don't remember."

We stood there a minute on Madison Avenue, letting the other people brush past us.

"Anyway," Heidi said, "I woke up, and Al was there,

whining her head off, and the rest of you were gone. So I took a bath and pulled myself together. I wanted it to be a dream. I tried all day to make it a dream."

"It sounds more like a warning."

"Don't." Heidi quivered. "Don't even think about it."

We were at the Seventy-third Street corner now. It dawned on Al that the walk was almost over, so she picked a spot off the curb. Heidi scooped.

It had been a long day. At least we had Heidi back, but it didn't solve everything. I climbed into bed that night, bushed, and tried to make my mind a complete blank. Which was probably not the best idea in the world.

When I pulled the sheet up, I knew I'd gotten more sun on the boat ride than I thought. I was glowing and beginning to itch. My mind got away from me and went back to the Circle Line tour. We'd gone down the Hudson River and past Governor's Island. When we'd sailed under the Brooklyn Bridge, the cars had hummed across it overhead.

That did it. My mind shifted gears, and I got this whole different view of Brooklyn Bridge. It seemed to loom out of an old, yellowed postcard. Now it was a new bridge, fresh paint on the cables, no rust on the stones. The traffic was cable cars and beer wagons and people on foot. They had on long skirts and shawls and top hats. Now they were moving, jerking into action, and it was all happening. On a cold gray day, the snow had turned to rain, nothing like our Sunday.

I could see all around: the bridge traffic, chunks of ice the size of houses in the river, smoke hanging over the low city. But I was in bed, and how often do you know you're in bed when you're having a regular dream? So it was more than that—a double negative. I was on the brand-new Brooklyn Bridge, but also in bed, hearing the silence of the house. No voices drifted in from the hall, and this was as alone as I'd ever been.

A funeral procession was coming back over the bridge. Two empty hearses with glass sides and then a closed carriage with the windows blacked out. All the horses were black, with black plumes on their heads. The cable cars stopped dead as they passed. The drivers were trying to hold back the hearse horses because they were heading home to their stables, trying to hurry. They were past me now, and I was standing at the other end of the bridge where Brooklyn begins.

Horsecar tracks cut through the cobblestones and piles of gray slush. Women picked their way along, holding up their splashed skirts. Kids stamped in the puddles. The wetness seeped into the shoes I seemed to be wearing.

I was looking for something up and down these Brooklyn streets. I was nearly running, past meat markets where whole carcasses were laid out, bleeding, on marble. I walked for miles till the houses began to have

yards with snow drifted against fences and pale crocuses poking up.

Nobody was around, but I heard a singing in the
wind, maybe the sea. I came to a gate at the end of a
street, a high arch with a stone angel kneeling on top. I
knew this was the place even before I walked through
the gates and saw graves.

Wreaths covered two graves together. The flowers
were black against the glaring snow. The wind turned
the ribbons, and I saw the letters on them. The wind
screamed and kept turning the wreath ribbons for me
to read.

IN LOVING MEMORY

FROM YOUR GRIEVING

MOTHER AND FATHER

I tried not to look, but a wreath lay just at my feet,
smaller and plainer:

MY DEAREST FRIENDS

GONE BUT NOT FORGOTTEN

BY ONE YOU LEAVE BEHIND

MAMIE

My eyes were blurring, but there was a wreath at the
top, bigger than the rest, woven with lilies:

PROFOUND CONDOLENCES

THE EBERSOLE FAMILY

I looked up at the two new gravestones. They were old-fashioned stones, but the chiseled words were crisp and new:

EMILY DUNLAP	TYLER JEREMIAH DUNLAP
May 4, 1873–	January 6, 1870–
March 12, 1888	March 12, 1888
"Safe from the Tempests of this World"	"Called Away in All His Bright Promise"

The wind screamed now, inside my head. The sky broke above me, and the rain, almost as warm as spring, pounded down on the wreaths. My face was wet with it.

Thirteen

The room began to form around me. My face was still wet, and my feet were numb from the slushy snow. But I was in bed, with daylight at the windows. It was an iron bed in a spare room of the Dunlaps' house. A bunch of sparrows were using the foot of the bed as a perch, making a racket. I sat up and saw my own face, surprised and wobbly, in the mirror of an old-time dresser. So I hadn't gotten all the way back to the present. But somehow I knew I was supposed to be here.

The curtains were fluttering rags because the wind had blown out the windows. The room was drifting with snow, and the birds chattered with the cold. When I pushed back the old patchwork quilt, it broke and split.

I don't know why, but my clothes were in the same pile where I'd left them last night when this was my room. Now an old braided rug was under them. Because of all the broken glass I reached for my sneakers first and shook out my shirt.

Luke was standing down by the stairwell when I looked out in the hall. He was shaking with cold, but dressed. He even wore a New York Mets ball cap Dad had bought him on the boat yesterday. He was standing there in the ruined third-floor hall of the Dunlaps' house with 1888 all around us. Al was at his feet, pulling back from everything. They were waiting for me.

"I figured that time would run out," he said. His teeth chattered, and there was something wild in his eyes. The cables of the old elevator hung down through the empty house. The striped paper was pulling off the walls.

"Look at this place. It's a dead place. Everybody's died, or gone away because they couldn't stand to live here. Are we going to let this happen?"

"Hasn't it happened already, Luke?"

But he shrugged that off. "Remember the voices we heard right from the first night, Chad? They were Tyler's and Emily's. You know that. Do you hear them now?"

All I heard was the sparrows' sound now that they'd taken over the hulk of Emily's house.

"Come on." Luke slipped his freezing hand into mine. As we walked down through the house, the wind died out. One landing down I saw the elevator cables weren't there anymore. Down on the second floor Emily's door was gone—just smooth paint. Now we were walking on oyster-white wall-to-wall carpeting. I heard the quiet hum of central air. When we came to the front hall, the bird cage elevator/phone booth was there in place. From the kitchen Mom was yelling up for Heidi to get out of bed. Summer-morning sun crept in. We were back to normal, whatever that is.

We turned to go down to the kitchen, and Luke

looked up at me from under his ball cap. "I think that was our last warning," he said. "I hated those graves, didn't you?"

Mom and Dad were racing around the kitchen, running late. Dad was dressed for the office. Mom and Jocelyn's mom and Heidi and Jocelyn were to meet early to be there first for an early-summer sale at Bergdorf's.

"I'm telling you the truth," Mom said. "It takes all my energy to get Heidi out of her room."

Luke and I selected a couple of muffins and left. "No Al," he said as we went out of the house, leaving her to sulk. But we didn't go farther than the stoop. We sat out there, and I watched him picking all the blueberries out of his muffin while we both wondered what the next move was.

"Doggone it, Chad," he said, "we're so close to knowing what we need to know. All we need is a little nudge."

Mom and Dad came out of the door above us. "I give up on Heidi," Mom said. "I'm just going to let her rot in that room. Honestly, if I'd been that moody at her age, my mother would have—"

"On the other hand," Dad said, "she was beginning to turn into a hippie punkstress, or whatever they call them. I'm glad she gave that up."

They almost fell over Luke and me.

"You two look so serious," Mom said, hovering. "Do you have enough to do today?"

"Plenty," we both said. As soon as they turned the corner, Luke was on his feet, pulling up his socks. "I guess we better go visit that Miss Hazeltine."

"Who? The crazy old Doberman lady? You've got to be kidding."

He wasn't, and it may have made sense. We were looking for links, and she went back farther than any other living human. But I thought Luke was scraping the bottom of the barrel. "She's just across the street at number twenty-nine," he said.

"It's not even nine in the morning."

"She probably doesn't know the difference," Luke said. "Anyway, I noticed something about her. She's lonely."

Number twenty-nine was basically like ours, but you could just walk in the front door. There was a row of mailboxes and buttons under names, so the place was apartments now. Luke pushed the Hazeltine button.

The speaker squawked. "Stop ringing my bell, or I'll call the law."

"Miss Hazeltine?" I said. "It's Chad and Luke, your . . . neighbors."

The speaker crackled. "Did you bring your animal?"

"No, ma'am."

"Then you can come up. I'm at the top on the front."

We climbed all the way up through the house, and the place didn't look too good, battleship-gray paint slapped on the walls and a light bulb every so often.

There was a little round peephole in Miss Hazeltine's

door. Inside, she was unlocking locks all the way to the floor. Then she was standing there, the same eerie sight she'd been the other day, with the same nightgown and raincoat, which I guess took her everyplace she wanted to be.

"I hope we're not—visiting too early," I said, trying for polite.

She squinted. "Doesn't matter to me. I was going to take my babies out for their walk."

They took up the whole other end of the room, watching every move Luke and I made. Their ears were sharp points, and their big paws were splayed out on the floor. Miss Hazeltine did all her living in this room. A refrigerator stood next to a big barrel full of empty Alpo cans. She didn't seem to wonder what we were doing here. Luke may have been right about her being lonely.

"You can take off your cap," she said to him. "Do you like butter brickle ice cream?" Luke blinked. We found places to sit, and then we ate ice cream with her.

"Keep your guard up," she said as she passed out the dishes. "Fiona and Xerxes love butter brickle."

I guess it was a regular New York party. Miss Hazeltine told us how many times this building had been broken into and about all the teenaged muggers she'd turned her babies loose on.

Right from the beginning Luke kept looking at me and then at a certain place in the room, back and forth. It got on my nerves. She was telling us about an armed daylight robbery at Soup Burg when Luke broke in to say, "Have you lived here quite a while, Miss Hazeltine?"

"Only sixty-eight years," she said. She was sitting on a low pile of magazines—*House Beautiful*—and her legs stuck out of her nightgown. They looked like two skinny road maps, but she was having a pretty good time.

"I grew up in the sticks. But when I was a young woman, I came to New York to get a job and live in this house with my aunt. She was my mother's older sister."

"I see," Luke said. And his head was still darting back and forth. I had no idea what he was seeing. She had everything in here, even laundry hanging from a clothesline.

"My aunt never married, you see," Miss Hazeltine was saying. She lowered her voice. "She left me this house, which was the old family place. I had it cut up into apartments, and that's what I live on. Of course I don't want the tenants to know I'm the owner. Otherwise, they'd keep wanting things—like kitchen stoves and hot water. They'd dog me to death."

When Fiona and Xerxes heard the word *dog*, they jerked to attention, growling deep in their throats. They watched Luke as he set aside his ice cream and stood up. He went over to a table and picked up a picture of somebody in a little silver frame. "Was this your aunt?" He held up the picture so Miss Hazeltine could see.

"That's right," she said. "Everybody knew her at one time. She founded the Hunter College School of Social Work, you know—a true friend of the poor—and raised every penny of the money herself. She was very well connected. One of her friends was Miss Consuelo Ebersole, who endowed the school with fourteen million dollars. That's prewar dollars, real ones."

"I guess your aunt and Miss Ebersole haven't been with us for quite a long time," Luke said.

"My land, no," Miss Hazeltine said. "My aunt died in her sleep at eight-seven. And Consuelo Ebersole blew up on the *Hindenburg.* I thought everybody knew that. It was in all the papers. Neither one of them married."

Luke came over and showed the picture to me. It was of Mamie Vanderdonk. Mamie, not a lot older than when we'd known her. "Bingo," he said, very softly to me.

Then he turned back to Miss Hazeltine. "Well, we'd better be running along." When I got up, so did Fiona and Xerxes. At least they came up in crouches, and their shoulder muscles rippled like Rambo.

"Drop by anytime," Miss Hazeltine said. "My babies like you. If they didn't, you'd know it."

And we were out of there. Luke couldn't wait to get down all those stairs.

"Let's get this straight," I said. "Mamie Vanderdonk was Miss Hazeltine's aunt. And Mamie founded that social-work school with Consuelo's money."

Luke bobbed his head. He was really pounding down those stairs. "But the important thing is, Mamie didn't marry Tyler, and neither did Consuelo. Guess why."

". . . Because he died. And Emily died."

"They died together, on the same day," Luke said. "Remember the date on both their gravestones? We ought to concentrate harder on our dreams and pick up clues like that right away. We're losing valuable time."

"Listen, Luke, how come you and I are having the same dreams lately?"

We burst through the front door and down Miss Hazeltine's stoop. "Because it'll take us both to save them. We can't let them die. That's out." He hung a left at the corner. Now we were sprinting up Madison Avenue. "Think about those voices we heard, the midnight voices." He jogged in place, waiting for a light to change. "Tyler's voice. Emily's voice."

". . . They're in a prison," I said. "He tells her to think about the park, about being there on a warm day. She says her hands are blue. He slaps her, to keep her awake."

The light changed, and I worked to keep up. "Where are we headed?"

"The library. And we haven't got all day. I think it's happening. I can feel it happening." He looked up at the sun blazing over Madison Avenue. "There's a chill in the air."

The library, up on Seventy-ninth Street, wasn't far

from where the old Ebersole mansion used to be. It was pretty impressive, like a castle. We hit the checkout desk at our top speed. A woman peered down at us over the counter. "We'd like to look at an old copy of the *Sun* newspaper," Luke said, "like 1888."

"I'm afraid we only keep the *Times*," she said.

"We'll give it a shot," he said, and she led us upstairs to where the microfilms are. Actually, it was called the Ebersole Memorial Room. She ran a microfilm into the machine for us.

"Any particular date?"

"Try March twelfth," Luke said.

We watched *The New York Times* for 1888 flash past us. "This is curious," the woman said, gazing at the screen. "There's no issue of the *Times* for that date. Could it be they didn't print that day?"

Luke nudged me. "Try March thirteenth."

She zeroed in on it and left us alone. We edged onto the same chair and saw the front page headlines: big screamers glowing out of the screen.

STORM OF THE CENTURY, GALE OF AWFUL FURY
RAGING:
TWO FEET OF SNOW FALLEN AND STILL COMING

Luke leaned nearer till his bill was brushing back and forth across the screen. He sopped up every word.

80-MILE WINDS COMBINE WITH
RECORD TEMPERATURE PLUNGE
HUNDREDS MISSING AND FEARED DEAD

ROOFS COLLAPSE, WINDOWS OUT
REST OF COUNTRY CUT OFF FROM MANHATTAN

FOOD RUNNING SHORT,
EGGS NOW 35¢ A DOZEN AND CLIMBING

"Read on," Luke said, though I could hardly see
around him. "Get to the fine print."

PANIC IN MID-AIR:
FATAL CRASH ON THIRD AVENUE ELEVATED
LINE

Yesterday at the height of the freakish storm, a
downtown train with more than five hundred passengers slipped backwards on ice-covered tracks
and was struck from behind by a second train with
brakes rendered useless by the track conditions.

Passengers waiting at the 76th Street Station
viewed in horror the impending collision in which
a brakeman was killed and twenty passengers in-
jured. The thunderous crash was heard for many
blocks around as the two trains telescoped. All four
of the city's elevated lines remain closed.

"That's not it," Luke said. "Only one dead. A brakeman." Another front-page article was

BRIDGES CLOSED AND FERRIES IN ALL RIVERS ADRIFT

The plummeting temperatures and sudden ice formation of Sunday night that paralyzed the city placed all slips and piers out of commission.

A ferry thought to be carrying twenty-five passengers across the Hudson drew near its Cortlandt Street slip only to find the berth iced up. Returning to the Jersey side, the captain discovered the pier there in similar condition. The boat continues to drift, and signals that the passengers are all as well as can be expected.

A three-car train of the Brooklyn Bridge cable system jumped the tracks, victim of high winds, blocking all access. Pedestrians are now crossing the ice-locked East River on foot. At high tide a large number of "ice-walkers" found themselves on a loose floe drifting toward the open bay. Their fate remains unknown.

"Her hands were blue with cold," I said, about Emily.

"But she and Tyler weren't with a bunch of people on a chunk of ice," Luke said. "They were alone." He sat back, not flipping on to see the inside pages. It was dark here in the Ebersole Room, except for the microfilm light. "It was a killer storm," he said, "like nobody had ever seen. It came up quick when they were expecting spring. It caught people off guard and—"

He froze. I guess that's the word. Then he slipped down from the chair, looking around for a way out of here. "Let's go," he said. "I know where they are."

Out in the hall we saw that the fluorescent lighting was gone. There'd been some display cases of rare books under glass, but there wasn't a stick of furniture out here now. Maybe I'd noticed that the library had been built as somebody's house. Now it *was* somebody's house, not as fine as the Ebersoles', but just as old.

The floor was parquet wood. At the top of the stairs we could see down to the big front hall. Instead of the checkout desk there was a little round sofa and potted palm trees, frost-nipped. We came down the stairs. The house felt deserted, but you never know. A hatstand by the front door held a load of cloaks from another age.

"We'll need a couple of those," Luke said. "Look at the weather out there."

Outside the glass front door it was a wasteland of winter snow with more falling. The storm of the century, though not our century. Luke slipped one of the long capes off a hook, wrapped it around himself, and tucked it up in the waistband of his shorts. I put on another one.

"They won't need them," he said. "Whoever lives here is gone already." We walked out of the unlocked door, up to our ankles, then up to our knees.

You couldn't see anything, but the wind blew us east, away from where the park must be. The wind did incredible things with the snow. The drifts were higher on the stoops across the street. I've never been colder, and we could have used boots. It felt like a mile to the corner. Ghostly-gray people wrapped up to the eyes were trying to dig out and tunnel. Now we were heading back down Madison Avenue, hanging on to buildings.

"What if this is March thirteenth?" I yelled. "What if it's too late?"

We heard the boom then, a tremendous explosion from somewhere, muffled by the snow, but loud.

"That'll be those two elevated trains telescoping," Luke yelled back. "So it's the twelfth. Besides, it's got to be the twelfth. Because if it isn't, Emily and Tyler are already dead."

Fourteen

My hands were blue, and my L.A. Gear sneakers were coming unstuck. The wind pried at my cloak, and I saw we were pushing our luck. But Luke plowed on ahead, and you don't give up before your little brother does.

The telephone poles along Madison Avenue had fallen against houses, knocking out windows, bringing down awnings. A dead horse was still being buried in snow at the Seventy-sixth Street corner. I barely kept up. Luke's a bantamweight, so he could go over drifts I kept sinking into. A lot of stuff was flying around in the air, so I was trying to watch my head, and his.

I'd have missed Seventy-third Street. Soup Burg wasn't there, but Luke made a sharp right. The whole block on the Dunlaps' side was a white cliff. You couldn't see the stoop of their house or the parlor windows. The snow was above their second floor. Higher than that, I saw curtains flapping out of the broken panes in the window of my room. There was no way to get into the place. But Luke was jaywalking over the drifts, heading for the house. He found where the stoop ought to be. It was a ski jump. "We could get boards or something and dig." But it looked hopeless even to him. "Hoist me up."

The snow was a yard deep here. When I gave him a

boost, I thought he'd vanish down to his neck. But the wind had been driving this snow at eighty miles an hour. Here was snowpack like we'd never seen, not even at Big Bear. He could stand on this. He started scrambling up the slope like a little human fly, digging in as he went. If he fell, I'd never catch him so I started up, too, and the snow held me. The wind was in our favor, though it could shift and sweep us off. I looked up once, and he had a hand on a windowsill. It was my room. I looked down and decided not to do that again.

He had the window up. His cape flapped around his waving legs, and he was pitching inside. Then he reached back for me. I fell into the room. We were inside now, on the gritty floor. Even out of the wind it was so cold, I thought my nose would drop off. Luke sat there, gasping, but then he was out in the hall, looking around, sensing the Dunlaps' house.

There was something out there, gloom or something. A lone sparrow looked down from the top of a door frame. Two more sparrows were on the floor, dead with their claws turned up.

Luke peered over the railing, his eyes following the elevator cables. Looking down, I saw the dome of the elevator with the spike on top, bright in the grayness. Something was wrong. The elevator was in the wrong place. It was lower than the second floor, but not all the way down to the front hall.

We started down the stairs. On the second floor we were outside Emily's closed door. The dome of the elevator was right there, a little lower than the railing. It was stopped—jammed between floors. When Luke dropped on his hands and knees, he could look right down into it.

"They're in there," he said, quiet as doom. "Both of them. We've found our way back to them, Chad."

Now I was straining to see down through the bars. I was looking into Emily's face. When she'd lost consciousness and fallen, she'd wedged against the bars. She was wearing the cloak from the park on Christmas day. Her face was like wax, and her eyes were closed.

Tyler had fallen across her. At the last he'd tried to get his coat off to put around her. It was pulled off his shoulders. But the cold had caught up with him, and the fear, and being caged in this frozen house. The two of them were like statues carved on a tomb, cold and still. They'd hung here trapped in their last hours as the storm of their century tore through the house. The electricity had gone out and caught them here together. They'd waited to be saved, down through the years, till only their voices echoed. Finally, we'd heard.

"We've got to go for help," I said, though I was sure we were too late, maybe only by minutes.

"Who?" Luke said. "And how could anybody see us?"

He looked around, trying to think of something. The supports of the banister were hardwood and thick as tree trunks. Just beyond them the bars of the elevator were solid metal. I could picture Tyler throwing away his last energy trying to bend them.

"The dome," Luke said.

It was there, bulging up within reach. But it looked solid, soldered on. "We'd need an acetylene torch or something."

"Let's be sure."

He hiked up his cape and threw a sneaker foot over the railing. But I pulled him back. Then I was crouched on the elevator dome myself. It was polished, but there wasn't enough light to see details. I felt around the edge of it, a design of raised metal that felt like flowers. Why did they have to make everything so fancy in those days?

I touched a little round-headed screw with a frozen finger. It was smooth, so even a screwdriver wouldn't help, not that we had one. I worked it loose, and it dropped down with a clink. Luke was leaning over the banister, breathing on my neck. I found the next screw. It was tighter, but I had more strength in my hands from somewhere. I worked on to the next one, reaching around the spike. Luke moaned.

I looked around at him, and his mouth was clenched, so it hadn't been him. He ducked down for a look into the elevator. "He moved," Luke said. "Tyler moved."

They were alive under this dome, in their prison. Tyler was. I kept working, and Luke held his breath. One screw wouldn't budge. Then it would. I lost track of where I was. My hand moved on and found a tiny empty hole. I'd come back where I'd started. Maybe the dome would lift off if I'd get off it myself.

I scrambled back over the banister, and Luke and I got on opposite sides. We both tried to get holds on the dome, which was going to be heavy. As I counted to three silently, he watched my lips. On *three* I heard Emily moan. It had to be Emily. Luke and I never had that much strength again, separate or together, but the dome made a grating sound and moved. It was fitted down like a very tight lid on a very big can.

"Again," I said. We didn't have enough leverage. Luke's hands were sparrow-small. But now we could get our hands in under the lip of the dome. Two more heaves and—

Then we heard the sound, high in the house. A door banged. And it could have been the wind working loose the attic door. We heaved again and lifted the dome maybe a quarter inch, but at least it didn't sink down into place again.

We heard pounding feet then. It was terrifying. We could use all the help we could get, but these feet were pounding down from the attic—somebody, something. The dome wobbled in our hands, and the spike pointed like a finger. I almost let go because I had this overpowering urge to cut and run. I almost lost it.

The stairs shuddered with the sound, now on the floor above us, turning down the stairs. Luke whimpered. I looked up. I had to. Heidi was there, teetering on the step behind Luke. Yes, she'd come from the attic because she'd dug out that old lace ball gown again and was wearing it, hitched up for running. Her hair was a mess, and her face was still smeared with the Oxy 10 cream she sleeps in. She was even wearing her Camp Beverly Hills shirt she sleeps in when her shorties are in the laundry. She'd dressed in a big hurry. The shirt was one strange sight under her ball gown. You could just read CAMP above the lacy bosom of her dress. And behind her on the step, peering around her skirt, was Al, panting.

"Come *on*," Heidi said. "Get that lid thing off and move out of my way."

"Heidi, what—"

"Get it off. But if they see it being lifted off by unseen hands, what are they going to think? They can see me."

"They're unconscious," I said, straining like mad to keep the dome from slipping back. Luke was bent double over the banister and could go either way.

Heidi switched past him and bent over to look down in the elevator. "Tyler's coming to, thank heaven. But we've got to get them out of that thing. I swear, you two are slow as molasses."

"Who's there?" Tyler said, hollow, from the bottom of a pit.

Luke and I gave an almighty heave, and the dome came loose. It was lighter than it had seemed. He shoved it my way, and I staggered back with it. It rolled out of my hand, clanged down the stairs, and lolled on its spike on the landing.

Then I heard Emily's voice, faintly. "I thought of the

park, Tyler," she said, "the park on the warmest day of summer."

Heidi leaned over and peered down into the roofless elevator.

Tyler looked up and saw her. "Darling," he said.

Luke dropped back against the striped wall and mopped his face with his cloak. Heidi kept peering down into the elevator. She must have looked great to Tyler.

"Is there like a ladder or something I can put down for you?" she said.

Luke darted into Emily's room and brought back a little bentwood chair from her writing table. He handed it over to Heidi, who let it down through the opening where the dome had been. Down there Tyler struggled to his knees, lifting up Emily, making room for the chair. He could stand on it, and they could make their escape, with Heidi's help.

She was still reaching down, and now she turned her smeary face to me. "He kissed my hand," she breathed. "I can take it from here."

Luke smiled. Then he turned away down the hall, slumping along with his cloak trailing behind him. I followed. It was like a deep freeze in this place, and one more dead sparrow was about all I could handle. We were coming up on Tyler's room, or Heidi's.

A small figure huddled against the door, not human. Al, in fact. She was kind of whiny, with her head cocked and her big begging eyes watery and gleaming in the gloom. Luke put his hand down, and she checked it for treats. "Good dog, Al," he said. "You helped."

He turned the old oval knob on Tyler's door. A flash of warm light hit us, and we strolled into Heidi's room. Her bed was a mess. The sheets were dragged halfway to the door, like she'd just jumped up out of deep sleep. Al bounced up on the bed and down again, showing off.

"That's about how it happened," Luke said, unwinding his cloak. "Mom and Dad left. We cut out for Miss Hazeltine's and the library. And Al found Tyler and Emily trapped in the elevator. She came in here and woke up Heidi." He patted Al's head.

"And Heidi raced up to the attic because when she put on that old dress, Tyler and Emily could see her. She'd never have gotten them out without us, though."

Luke nodded. "I guess it was all meant to happen."

I got out of my cloak too. It was a nice, even seventy-six degrees in here. Noontime summer sun beamed in through Heidi's blinds across the Dame Barbara Cartlands in her bookshelf.

Luke was folding up our cloaks. "Well, anyway," he said, "we won't be hearing their voices anymore. At night."

"I guess not," I said, though maybe I didn't sound too relieved. "I liked Emily. A lot. But at my age they never seem to notice you back." And Luke just looked up at me because he hasn't gotten to that stage yet.

There was no way to return the cloaks, so we stashed them in Heidi's closet, where they may be yet. Then

Heidi herself rocketed into the room and banged the door shut behind her. The sound echoed through the house, and there was something final about it.

She was red faced and chilled to the bone, and she really wasn't looking her best. CAMP was still spelled out across her upper chest, and the bustle on her ball gown looked like it was trying to escape. Her breath came in short, sharp gasps.

"One question, Heidi," I said. "Just one."

"Like what?"

"You were very good at . . . all this. You deserve a lot of credit. Did you ever have any—unusual experiences before now?"

She looked away. "Not really," she said, hardly moving her lips. "Well, when I was little, I used to get up in the night and go down to the utility room back home and watch the Indians. But I don't think that counts."

Why am I always the last to know anything?

Heidi kind of wanted us out of her room, so we left, Luke leading the way. Out in the hall the oyster-white carpeting led to the stairwell, and everything was normal and now. You could hear the hum of central air-conditioning, and somehow the whole place felt good. That's the way with houses, if there are always families looking after them down through the generations. A house needs love just like anybody else.

I was still a little dazed that day, but it seemed like our whole lives, Heidi's and Luke's and mine, had been leading us to this particular house. It seemed like we'd

been gearing up our whole lives to save Emily and
Tyler so they could go on living in their time. I didn't
even wonder why it had happened to us, but I knew
we'd opened our last door to the past here. And I guess I
was glad.

I wouldn't forget Emily, but I figured we'd never
have word of her or Tyler again. I figured wrong.

Fifteen

Our second week in New York was completely different —more like we'd expected. Dad and I did some early-morning runs. Then later in the day Luke and I would go back to the park with Al to let her chase around and eat grass. Mom met Mary Lou for lunch a couple times. But Heidi eased off on Jocelyn, who she said was basically a fashion victim. Our whole family went out to Shea for a Mets game. We took the subway and ate junk food in the stands. And we watched them cream the dreaded Astros.

But it wasn't like nothing ever happened. I was still careful going through doors, and we never went near the attic. Whenever the phone rang, I let somebody else answer because it was in the brass bird cage phone booth thing at the bottom of the stairs.

Once in a while I'd wake up in the night, wondering if something woke me. I'd lie there hearing the sounds of an old house and watching the streetlights play on my ceiling. I'd catch myself listening for their voices, Emily's voice. She never came near my dreams in those nights. In fact I was beginning to dream myself back onto a Honda Gyro. But I'd try to imagine Emily growing up, becoming a young lady, then an older lady, entering our century. Things like that, but I never heard her voice again. She faded, though not from my thoughts.

Then our New York trip was over surprisingly fast. On that last morning Luke and I took Al out for one final New York walk, and she knew what was coming next. She remembered the plane ride, traveling as baggage. When we came back, the suitcases were in rows in the front hall, and we were going to need two cabs.

We were all downstairs, having a last look around. "One thing I never got used to," Mom said, "were those framed dots over the fireplace."

Then we heard somebody slip a key into the front door. We all looked, and the door opened a crack. A big hand came in and fumbled along the wall, to turn off the burglar alarm. Dad recovered quickest and pulled the front door open. Three people were out on the stoop, surprised. They were a man and a woman and their son, a guy of about seventeen or so. Heidi quivered.

"Oh," the woman said. "We had no idea."

They were nice-looking people, so we all moved up behind Dad.

"We thought you might be off to the airport by now," the man said. "But take your time, by all means."

"You must be the owners of the house," Dad said.

"That's right." There was a jumble of luggage and tennis rackets behind them on the stoop. "We're the Dunlaps."

Luke blinked. So did Heidi. I could hear my own breathing. Al went over and smelled their shoes.

"Our plane came in early," the lady—Mrs. Dunlap—said. "We don't want to get in your way. We live only on the top two floors anyway."

Luke nudged me, hard.

But Mom came forward, and we all introduced ourselves. They were Mr. and Mrs. Jerry Dunlap and their son, Ty. When he met Heidi, he gave her a really appreciative look. Small sparks flew between them.

The Dunlaps would have gone on upstairs, but Mom wanted them to look over the part we'd rented to make sure everything was in good shape. She'd practically hosed down the kitchen, and she wanted credit for it.

I offered to help Ty bring in their luggage and carry it upstairs. Luke was right there with us, and I for one had a little trouble imagining what was coming next.

Ty looked like he might have made the wrestling team at some hard-to-get-into prep school. He said they'd spent two weeks at Hilton Head, and he'd be a senior at Trinity. We were hustling two suitcases apiece up the stairs with Luke on my heels. Up on our floor Ty fumbled a key out of his pocket and slipped it into the padlock on that door to the little staircase that leads to the top of the house.

We started up behind him. It was stuffy up here, unaired. I thought of the girls in aprons and the plaster off the walls. I thought ahead to the attic another flight up, with the hobbyhorse that eyed us, and the old trunk.

"Home again," Ty said on the fourth floor, where the maids had lived—Pegeen and the others. "We've got a duplex arrangement."

The whole floor opened up into a big living room across the front of the house. Really good furniture, deep carpeting, track lighting throughout. There was an open-plan kitchen-dining area behind. It hadn't been maids' rooms for years.

"My room's at the front of the old attic. Come on up."

He had a nice layout up there with a lot of superior sound equipment, a word processor, and his own bathroom separate from his parents'.

"You wouldn't think it was ever an attic, would you?" he said, and you wouldn't.

Luke strolled over to a front window where he'd be able to look straight across into Miss Hazeltine's windows. And above that over to the tower of the Carlyle Hotel. It wasn't hard to tell what he was thinking—that if it hadn't been for us, this would still be an old deserted attic. Or maybe the house wouldn't even exist. Ty wouldn't exist. Luke stood there at the window, deep in thought.

When we got back downstairs, Mom and Dad and Heidi were sitting around the living room with the Dunlaps.

"The top two floors are plenty of space for the three of us," Mrs. Dunlap was saying. "We often rent out the lower part, but always to people we know. But we just got the sudden idea of renting through an agency this time. I'm so glad you happened to get it."

"So are we," Mom said.

"And I hope you like the art." Mrs. Dunlap gestured to the framed dots over the fireplace. "I dabble, and it's my own work."

"Stunning," Mom said.

"I wish you were staying longer," Mr. Dunlap was saying to Dad. "I'd like to show you my club—full Nautilus. I hope you were comfortable here. No trouble with the house?"

Mrs. Dunlap raised an eyebrow at her husband. On the collar of her dress she wore a small pin with pearls and an emerald—a family heirloom, no doubt. "Now, Jerry," she said, "you're not going to go into that old story, are you?"

Luke was on the arm of Mom's chair, taking everything in. "What old story?" he asked.

"Oh, it's about this house," Mrs. Dunlap said, "kind of a tradition."

"Is it haunted?" Luke said, making big eyes to encourage her.

"Nothing like that. Not really."

Ty was there with one elbow propped on his mother's chair, grinning—mostly at Heidi. And she was looking at him like Tom Cruise had come to life. Sometimes I can read Heidi.

"You know these old New York houses—so much

going on down through the years," Mrs. Dunlap said. "And Jerry's family have lived here—how long, Jerry?"

"Well over a century," he said, "since before the Great Storm of eighty-eight."

"Come on, Mother," Ty said, "tell them about the Ghost Lady on the Stairs, the Mystery Lady."

"Now, Ty, you know there's nothing to that. We never saw her or heard her or anything."

Mom looked around the room, like maybe we'd rented more than we bargained for.

"It's an old tale told in my family," Mr. Dunlap said, "about my great-grandfather. Ty here is named for him. It seemed that as a young man he nearly married Consuelo Ebersole, the heiress, which would certainly have improved the fortunes of our family."

"Consuelo blew up on the *Hindenburg*," Luke offered, but then he's a bright kid, always coming up with something.

"That's right," Mr. Dunlap said. "But one night at a party the Ebersoles gave, Great-grandpa Tyler met another girl, a girl nobody knew. Legend has it that she was incredibly beautiful."

Heidi stirred.

"So that was the end of him as far as Consuelo Ebersole was concerned."

"But what's that got to do with your stairway?" Luke said, helping the story along.

"Soon after," Mr. Dunlap said, "the Great Storm struck—worst storm ever recorded in New York. Ty's parents were over in Jersey that Sunday evening and couldn't get back home. They were on a Hudson River ferryboat. The servants had all gone to look after their relatives. Tyler and his sister were alone in the house, getting ready to take flight themselves."

"You will have noticed the phone booth in the hall," Mrs. Dunlap remarked. "It was one of the earliest elevators. They made the mistake of getting into it together, and they were trapped in it when the electricity failed."

"But they didn't die," Luke said.

"Well, no," Mrs. Dunlap said. "I expect the truth is that the electricity came back on, and they got themselves out. Which is a good thing, considering that Jerry's a direct descendant. That storm might have put a sudden end to the Dunlap family."

"But the legend is a lot more colorful," Mr. Dunlap said. "The story is that the beautiful girl reappeared—in the same gown she'd worn at the Ebersoles' ball—and rescued them both. Vanishing again, of course. And that's the story of the ghost on our stairs. I have to say, she's very quiet as ghosts go."

Heidi sat there silent as the tomb.

"You know how these old families are," Mrs. Dunlap said, "full of tales that grow taller with the years."

Though she never tore her eyes off Ty, Heidi managed to speak. "But who did Tyler marry?"

Mrs. Dunlap glanced over at her husband. "That's an

authentic part of the Dunlap family history and something of a scandal at the time."

"Great-grandpa Tyler married the parlor maid!" Mr. Dunlap said. "Her name was Pegeen. My father remembered her. She turned into a real old aristocrat over the years and ruled the whole family with a rod of iron. My grandfather was their eldest son. They had three more sons and a daughter who appeared to be just as feisty as her mother, old Pegeen. She married a man named MacPherson in defiance of them all and went out west with her husband and was never heard from again."

By now the room seemed to be going around and around. "You said Tyler had a sister?" I said. "The one in the elevator?"

"Ah, yes. She became the family celebrity. She was Emily, duchess of Castleberry. She married into the British peerage and was a great friend to the Royal Family. She lived through the London Blitz and died at a great age. Had a very fine home in the English countryside, too, I believe, with gardens now open to the public."

But it was getting to be time to go because we had a plane to catch. We said our good-byes to the Dunlaps, and they told us to keep in touch. We made our plane and checked Al through to California.

It was a pretty routine flight. We flew between the clouds and the sun with nothing but deep blue sky up there. I dozed, and once when I was dropping off I thought I caught a glimpse of Emily. She was standing in a garden with everything in bloom. Shading her face was a big old straw gardening hat she'd probably had for years. On her arm was a basket of flowers. It was a warm day in England or someplace like it under a deep blue sky. She was just there for a moment. Then she was gone.

With the three-hour time difference we were back at El Rancho Bravo before dark. Al shot in the front door under our feet, barking like mad and practically turning backflips. The house looked different: bigger or smaller or something—the way home does when you get back.

Heidi was on that phone quicker than you can believe, to tell Melissa about Ty Dunlap, this great guy she met in New York, who'd make chopped liver out of any Thor Desmond.

She was still on the phone when the rest of us were unpacked. Mom and Luke and I were sitting around the family room drinking lime Calistoga water, which you can't get in New York. I was just wondering what happened to Dad when he came into the room. He was back in sweatpants and UCLA shirt, his California uniform. He was also carrying the family Bible, kind of an odd combination.

"Something's been haunting me all the way home," he said.

The word *haunting* managed to get Luke's attention, and mine.

"Look at this." Dad opened the Bible on the table in front of us. His family tree was written in on the front page. Each generation was added in different handwriting, faded now. "Ever since Mr. Dunlap mentioned he had a relative who married a man named MacPherson, I've been thinking about my grandmother up in Petaluma. I hardly remember her, but she was my mother's mother, and the name was MacPherson. Look, here it is."

We looked, back past Dad's entry and his mother's to

Alicia Dunlap MacPherson
born New York City, 1892

"I didn't remember her maiden name was Dunlap, but my grandfather was a MacPherson, and I thought they'd come out from the East."

"For heaven's sake," Mom said. "What did they say about her? Was she the daughter of the man in the elevator and the maid? Something like that."

"Which would mean that Dunlap and I are descended from the same great-grandparents," Dad said. "But I don't know. Twelve million people in New York, and we end up in the house of long-lost cousins? Who'd believe it?"

Luke, for one. I can tell what he's thinking sometimes, and this was one of the times. I thought he and I might just as well get out on the driveway where we could shoot some hoops, just on our own. Anyway, he needs the practice. He dribbles real slow and higher than his head.

Outside, I said, "It looks like Heidi had a crush on her own great-great grandfather."

"And let's see," Luke said, "that would make Emily your aunt about three times removed."

I'd passed him the ball, and he made a lucky shot from the center line. "But the important thing is," he said, "we weren't just saving their lives. We were saving our own. It's a good thing for us we came along."

And basically, I knew what he meant. He retrieved the ball, dribbled it high, and went for another lucky shot, even though it was evening now, and you could hardly see the hoop.

ABOUT THE AUTHOR

RICHARD PECK is one of the most highly acclaimed and popular writers of fiction for young adults. He attended Exeter University in England and holds degrees from DePauw University and Southern Illinois University. His novels for young people include *Remembering the Good Times, Are You in the House Alone?, Father Figure, Secrets of the Shopping Mall, Close Enough to Touch,* and the four novels starring Blossom Culp and Alexander Armsworth. Three of Mr. Peck's novels have been filmed for television, and his most recent novel for Delacorte Press is *Those Summer Girls I Never Met.*

Richard Peck lives in New York City.